FORGETFULNESS

FORGETFULNESS

MICHAEL MEJIA

FC2
NORMAL/TALLAHASSEE

Published by FC2 with support provided by Florida State University, the Publications Unit of the Department of English at Illinois State University, and the Florida Arts Council of the Florida Division of Cultural Affairs. This project is supported in part also by an award from the National Endowment for the Arts, which believes that a great nation deserves great art.

Address all inquiries to: Fiction Collective Two, Florida State University, c/o English Department, Tallahassee, FL 32306-1580

ISBN: Paper, 1-57366-122-8

Library of Congress Cataloging-in-Publication Data
Mejia, Michael, 1968-
Forgetfulness / by Michael Mejia.— 1st ed.
    p. cm.
  ISBN 1-57366-122-8
  1. Webern, Anton, 1883-1945—Fiction. 2. Vienna (Austria)—
Fiction. 3. Composers—Fiction. 4. Monologues. I. Title.
  PS3613.E444F67 2005
  813'.6—dc22

                              2005001348

Cover Design: Lou Robinson
Book Design: Tara Reeser

Produced and printed in the United States of America
Printed on recycled paper with soy ink

NATIONAL
ENDOWMENT
FOR THE ARTS

FOR

———————————————

MINDY AND MY FAMILY

TABLE OF CONTENTS

What could be even more fascinating than the suspense as to what the place which I have so often imagined will look like? The suspense of how I restore my imagination after I have seen the place.

—Karl Kraus

VARIATIONS: ANTON WEBERN
1883-1945

If twenty clocks are hanging on one
wall and you suddenly look at them,
every pendulum is in a different place,
they all tell the same time and yet don't,
and the real time flows somewhere in
between. This can have an uncanny
effect.

—Robert Musil

The *eye*, acquiring cyclopean proportions when seen reversely through the magnifying glass before it, is not still. It makes no grand or deliberate transits in any particular direction but it appears to be trained on a single object or isolated region. Its incremental and seemingly random shifts, then, are most likely involuntary. These are so minute, in fact, that at any lesser level of observation than this, they should not be considered motion. Rather, it might be said that the *eye* quivers in spite of itself, with life and in spite of life, in spite of the same life force that has trained it on its narrow field, that has mandated that it hold still and focus for the purpose of close observation, scrutiny, single-minded study. The *eye* quivers in a way that resembles the visibly unstable state of a still pool of liquid, struggling to maintain its stillness.

The gray-blue *iris*, like a soft sea-creature beneath the aquarian dome of the *cornea*, also moves, though with a more calculated exactitude than the greater ocular structure. It moves economically and without caprice, as does the geometer. The circle at the center of the *iris*, the dark void known as the *pupil*, appears to be moving, but, in fact, the inside edges of the *iris*'s striated membrane are contracting and relaxing, varying the magnitude of light information allowed to stream through the *eye*'s *lens* and into the *posterior chamber*, to disperse through and illumine the thick jelly of the *vitreous body*, to bombard the *retina*'s millions of *photoreceptors*.

All of this happens now.

The *photoreceptors* of this *eye* are fully operational, capturing an unending stream of data, light information—fragments, particles of form and color, distance and size—assembling a model of the world (of the object of observation, the isolated region) and sending it on for processing, recording, and analysis. For appreciation.

It may be noted that the *iris*'s subtle movements also seem to encompass a number of additional corrections of the *pupil* in response to movements of the magnifying glass itself, as the latter is not wholly immobilized.

A two-dimensional, peach-colored polygon of light appears on the wet surface to one side of the *iris*, on the outside curve of the red-veined white of the eye, or *sclera*. A faint double of this same figure glistens on the outside curve of the *cornea*. The polygon, like the *pupil*, is subjected to continuous, though less precise, transformations, mutations, not solely because of the micromotions of the eye and magnifying glass—or rather of the hand presumed to be holding the magnifying glass—but most likely because of an unseen changeable object or set of objects partially obscuring the source of the light: the branch of a tree, a passing cloud, a gradually lifting fog.

> Colors are the deeds of light, what it does and what it endures. In this sense we can expect them to tell us something about light.
>
> —Johann Wolfgang von Goethe

Summer's passing becomes tangible in the gradually diminish- Maiernigg
ing warmth of successive afternoons, in the slow and silent deto-
nation of color in the leaves, the final leap of a dying flame. One
may also observe it in the transformations of gestures and dis-
positions of southern folk, as if flora themselves, maintaining by
slight corrections the organic equilibrium of the Austrian countryside, conserving energy now in anticipation of the change of
seasons. The northerly breeze becomes visible, scarlet, tangled
in the hand-dyed trim of a white tablecloth. The heavy dynam-
ics of warm milk in a rough wooden pail. Thick hands wipe the
beard and moustache clean, the knuckles stiff and cracking like
nutshells. Pink and chafing fingers pinch the dough. At sunrise,
at the first bells, at the last bells, a broad and nasal utterance is a
family almanac, classifying the sunlight, unspooling a continuum
of knowledge, a millennial period of symbol and ritual, of
agronomy and husbandry, of faith and deep silence, of generations of men, crops, and animals grown up, torn and fragmented,
scattered among the windbreaks and thickets, the green and
muddy cradles of the stream- and pondbeds, stone fences,
stumps, and creeping shadows. The mountain achieves another
centimeter and with a thunderous crack, rending ice and stone,
announces itself. A collective shudder descends from the peaks,
rolls across the valley. Metal on metal is the sound of the cows'
bells, the glacial retreat and advance of the herd.

From the slope above the village of Maria Wörth, a young
hiker, Anton von Webern, watches the shifting light on the
surface of the shivering Wörthersee, the small flotillas of cloud
shadows colliding and separating, the gleaming swans and
dark geese gliding near shore. A thinning fleet of holiday
sails tacks back and forth around the slender peninsula in
and out of the cool, pointed shadow of the church. The broad

white hulls sweetly pitch and yaw to the rhythms of military bands and barrel organs, the languid crews piqued and annoyed by the buzzing of three overfull and careless little motorboats. The scented shoreline promenade has begun, and the penultimate late-summer pleasure hovers unsteadily aloft above its silvered double in the lake, as if supported by invisible arcades of opposing magnetisms, all of it fading softly, irrevocably into the haze.

Chatterings in the treetops. The swift forms of two birds. A rustling, a bump, a rattling. Young Webern turns in time to see a tiny shadow scrambling down the roof of Gustav Mahler's forest hut before leaping, fearless, into the trees.

He stands at the closed window.

He enters through the lattice doors.

He rests his palm on the cool, dusty table.

The tabletop is solid, scarred, and stained with ink. There is a wooden chair. An empty shelf. A cold stove. Four marks on the floor where an upright piano once stood. The air is dank, cavelike, with no lingering scent of life. No hair. No warmth. No thread. The mountain is here, and the southern countryside, rising like a fog from beneath the floor, creeping in through every chink, every open orifice. Dust in the corners, moss and mold in the crevices. A slow invasion of forest life as new owners prepare to dine on the sun-gilded terrace of the summer house below, the former Villa Mahler.

Involuntary spells of memory can raise the dead. Their first meeting, in Vienna, after a concert of Mahler's lieder organized by Schönberg. Mahler's departure for New York from the

Westbahnhof, the gatherings of friends and students in homes and taverns when he returned. Who would speak when he spoke: his ideas, the depth of his thought on composition, on art overwhelming even Schönberg—the forgotten mastery of Bach, the model of Nature in counterpoint, the development of a work from a single cell, the vital importance of variation, the unique beauty of Schubert's melodies. He had an irregular walk, a graceful shabbiness. The demon of the opera in pince-nez. His soft, thoughtful, eastern eyes and the timbre of his *here, please, of course.* For a few summers this space was the garden of his genius.

The hair rises. The air freezes in the throat, burns the tips of the ears.

Something in the ether struggles toward life, a little storm of will, singing with visions: mountain ranges, glaciers, the high alpine meadows, Vienna, a light breeze in the high grass, brooding eastern provinces, vast America, a thousand manifestations of love like hieroglyphics, agony, his own heart, the footprints of children, the black Atlantic, a helmetless hero and an immense forward motion, the labyrinthine, *Wunderhorn* forest, a moonlit pool full of lilies, the contemplative joy of an imagined Asia, delicate vegetable structures, the hammer and the military drum, a shadow on the moon, the shroud of a child, the voices of the world in impossible union, and—as the soul drifts away—herd bells in the valley. The world, the constellations, the universe left behind, vibrating with unanswerable longing.

A face in the trees: the remains of a scarecrow.

No one at the window, no one at the door. A nightingale sings darkness into the trees.

Anton von Webern stands alone at the table, shivering, fearful. He reaches out to touch a solid thing. As the soul drifts away.

The lowing of cattle and the laughter of country men. Herd bells. Simple, empty, metal shells.

Monday at 6 o'clock I have to go to a *Mahler celebration* in the Opera. They are setting up the Rodin bust in the foyer.

—Anton Webern, letter to Hildegard Jone and Josef Humplik, 16 May 1931

Lohengrin   —Ladies and gentlemen, we apologize for our technical difficulties. As you know, it's a new production this season and...

Loud squawks and honks from offstage. The audience laughs.

—Yes, well, we've had, we've not had quite enough time to...yes...well. We'll get underway shortly I'm sure.

More honks. More laughter. The emperor's box is empty.

—Just a moment.

The stage manager makes a move toward the wings, then turns to the conductor.

—Would you...would you, please, Herr Direktor Weingartner?

The orchestra begins to play the first act overture again. Shouts from stage left.

Movement in the boxes. Movement on the floor. People begin to head out into the salons.

—Weingartner's Follies, grinning Oskar grouses to Tilly, loud enough to pique those around them.

—I'm going to walk about, I think. Will you come?

The stage manager returns waving his arms.

—Please, please, ladies and gentlemen, do sit down, we've almost got it!

—All their rage to undo Mahler, Oskar says. The Herr Maestro recircumcizing Wagner, but a proper Christian operation this time, eh? Dr. Weingartner's program of desemitization to please these...

Their pink, fleshy heads turn in anticipation.

—Swine.

—Shall we? Tilly asks.

Another shout from offstage and a perfect swan emerges, flapping its wings wildly, streaking toward the top of the house. Heads turn, look up. The bird wheels around the grand chandelier, and the crowd begins to cheer and applaud until shit rains down on them. They scramble when the swan dives toward the floor, gasp when it rises again, fall silent and lower their heads as it slams into the ceiling and spirals dead to the floor amid a shower of gold paint and plaster.

After a brief commotion in the pit, an eager cellist throws the cover off the rehearsal piano and plays Siegfried's funeral music. A white uniformed colonel and his adjutant solemnly bear the broken bird to the stage where the weeping stage manager covers the swan with his coat and, staggering, disappears into the wings.

Oskar nearly chokes trying to suppress his laughter, lets out a hoot when Tilly pinches him. She points at something and Oskar looks up to see, through the humid haze of the third-floor standing area, someone waving at him, shapeless hat in hand, less a greeting than a naive desire to be recognized. The sour, uncomfortable expression, the familiar, penetrating gaze of the young man from Braunau.

Theater and military procedure indeed
have much in common. I try to make ev-
erybody take things as seriously as possible. The relevance of everything is explained, even if it looks like mere drill.
The best of sense really governs each detail. That sense they are to comprehend.

—Anton von Webern, letter to Arnold
Schönberg, 8 June 1915

1916   Perhaps it was like this:

On the morning you were informed of your fitness for front-line service, you taped diagrams on the wall outside the barracks and dismantled the machine, a Schwarzlose 1907. You rinsed out the cooling jacket as cautiously as if you were washing your little boy. You cleaned and oiled the close-fitting arms and valve covers, the screws and nuts, the massive return spring.

You cleared the tubes for oil and steam and water. You rammed a cloth through the barrel.

Did you stand back then and admire the various parts glistening in the midsummer sun, laid out in the order prescribed?

It is probable that the sky was clear, the air cool and fresh, and that the sun's intensity was magnified by this atmosphere of purity, its waves of radiation visibly warping the air, waves achieving a certain audibility, the buzz of process, of transmutation.

Through the barracks's open windows the young boys under your command from Leoben and Graz, from mountain villages and farmsteads might have been heard laughing together at their earnestly intoned fairytales of fucking the milkmaid, the servant girl, the older sister's friend. Or perhaps they were baiting the Slovenian, Janez, into a brawl in the paddock. Or perhaps they were playing chess or whist, or singing a melancholy harvest song accompanied by a zither.

[A]bout 1911 I wrote the "Bagatelles for String Quartet" (Op. 9), all very short pieces, lasting a couple of minutes—perhaps the shortest music so far. Here I had the feeling, "When all twelve notes have gone by, the piece is over." Much later I discovered that all this was a part of the necessary development.... In short, a rule of law emerged; until all twelve notes have occurred, none of them may occur again.

—Anton Webern, *The Path to Twelve-Note Composition*, Lecture V, 1932

But all this was beyond your notice, wasn't it? You were thinking ahead, weren't you, to the end of the war, toward a solution to the work you'd left undone?

Perhaps you set about reconstructing the machine gun then, holding up each part and turning it in your fingers, stroking with your thumb the beveled edges and graded surfaces, so queerly molded, great advances in Austro-Hungarian weapons engineering, near perfect, so you'd been told, in economy and efficiency.

On the metal's oily surface the sunlight opened, revealing the miracle of its prismatic spectrum, the hidden, eternal structure within the light.

Here, however, those who are wont to proceed according to a certain method may perhaps observe that we have as yet not decidedly explained what color is.... Therefore we have only to repeat that color is a law of nature in relation with the sense of sight.

—Johann Wolfgang von Goethe, *Theory of Colors*, 1810

Did you linger for very long over the weapon's components,

[J]ust as the researcher into nature strives to discover the rules of order that are the basis of nature, we must strive to discover the laws according to which nature, in its particular form 'man,' is productive. And this leads us to the view that the things treated by art in general, with which art has to do, are not 'aesthetic,' but that it is a matter of natural laws, that all discussion of music can only take place along these lines.... Since the difference between color and music is one of degree, not of kind, one can say

or did you move on quickly, retracing your steps? Did you return to where you'd begun, matching each part with its shape in the diagrams, then screwing it back into place? Did you hold them up, then screw them in, all in order, one, two, three?

that music is natural law as related to the sense of hearing.

—Anton Webern, *The Path to the
New Music*, Lecture I, 1933

Or perhaps you weren't even thinking about them as springs
or valve covers or screws, or about their specific contributions
to the objectives of speed and death. Perhaps it was only the
notion of order itself that was spread out, like the sunlight,
across your table. Perhaps they were simply objects with unknown functions demanding order, not the components of a
rational machine, but material events related to one another
through an as yet unarticulated technology, not a tool for the
defense of *heimat*, but a steel abstraction, a vehicle of transfor-
mation, a model of the lieder of the new age.

Here the musical solution to the much
contested problem of smashing the
atom has succeeded.

—*Neue Freie Presse*, review of Webern's
Piano Variations, Op. 27, 6 November
1937

But, dear Pepo, I also saw the Parthenon
Frieze! I stood there for an hour and a
half. It's an indescribable miracle. The
conception! It is the exact counterpart
of our method of composition: always
the same thing in a thousand forms.

—Anton Webern, letter to Hildegard
Jone and Josef Humplik, 3 May 1933

This is the concept of World.

Fragments in the walls, on the floors.

Some
cross
over to
other
slabs.

Let everyone be a Greek in his
own way, but let him be a Greek!

—Johann Wolfgang von Goethe

Is this history?

A procession.
A simple
repeated form.

Horses with riders,
chariots, men,
women, animals.

What has been lost?

Arms. Legs. The torso, the
tunic, the shield, the pitcher,
the pipes, the beckoning hand.

Is this allegory?

Faceless riders.
Horses without eyes.

Decoration depends on variety;
in writing and in buildings it
provides a change for the intellect and the eye, and when
decoration on architecture is
combined with simplicity, the
result is beauty: for a thing is
good and beautiful if it is what
it ought to be.

—Johann Joachim Winckelmann

Identical forms, but features
unique to each: speed, lazi-
ness, unruliness, intelligence,
anxiety, humor, pride, friendship, respect for position, respect for the gods, an impa-
tience for those lagging behind, an expectation that others will follow.

Some nude,
some clothed,
some helmeted,
others
bareheaded.

Beyond is blank stone.

Is this forgetfulness?

On a spring evening in Vienna, as the bells toll five o'clock, Dr. Florian Mittermayr, a music critic with political aspirations, enters the Café Sperl. He is greeted by Otto, an affable giant of a lisping, white-haired waiter. Otto's black suit and vest show few signs of wear.

Part I: Greetings!

—Good evening, Herr Dr. Mittermayr!

—Good evening, Otto.

—Would you like your usual seat?*

—Of course I would. Why would I not?

—Yes. And will you be dining here alone tonight, Herr Dr. Mittermayr?

—Yes. Yes. The old bitch is up at the sanatorium again.

Part II: Ordering Food and Drink

—I will fetch the menu.

—There is no need for a menu. What is the special?

—We have a very nice Chicken à la Marengo tonight, Herr Dr. Mittermayr.

—Chicken? Good God. Well, I suppose that will do.

—Wonderful! Would you like tea or coffee, Herr Dr. Mittermayr?

—A beer. Gösser.**

—Excellent!

---

* Always use the polite form, *Sie*, when addressing a superior or someone you don't know very well.

** In general it is considered more polite to say "please," *bitte*, when ordering something to eat or drink.

Otto nods politely and goes to check on a young woman in the corner who has been trying to attract his attention.

Part III: Compare and Contrast

Near the door, two women enjoy dessert.

—Do you like the Sachertorte, Hanna?

—Yes, I do. It is better than the Hotel Sacher's. And how is the pudding?

—I am afraid it is a bit thick. I prefer the strudel much better, though the Napoleon is also quite good.

Another woman approaches carrying a small box tied up with string.

—Hello, Hanna. Hello, Wilma.

—Good evening, Katrina. What is in your box?

—A cat. His name is Ludwig, but I call him Pickle. Pickle is a gift given to me by my neighbor, Dr. Schrödinger, from the university.

—How sweet. What kind of cat is it, dear? May we see him?

—Oh, no. I am sorry. Pickle may be dead.

—Heavens!

—He may also be alive. As long as I do not open the box, Pickle is both dead and alive.

—All at once?

—Yes! Isn't he adorable?

—Yes, my dear, yes! Pickle is very handsome! He has such unique and beautiful markings.

Part IV: Shock, Surprise, and Unpleasantness

Dr. Mittermayr stands, squinting at the newspaper rack. Another man, Dr. Karel Bilenski, a Bohemian veterinary surgeon, runs into him, almost toppling Dr. Mittermayr over his table.

—Damn you!

The large glass ashtray slides off Dr. Mittermayr's table and falls to the floor, bounces once, spins and glitters like a trout, then hits the floor again and shatters. Everyone stares.

—Excuse me! Ah!
—You damn… Ah!

The two men recognize each other.

—Florian!
—Karel! You are as clumsy as ever. Damn you!
—Please excuse me. Were you leaving?
—No. I was going to get a newspaper when you trampled me.
—I said excuse me.
—Yes.
—Yes.*

Part V: Express Your Opinion!

A young Czech student is unable to pay his bill. The cashier is annoyed by this and also by the student's poor German.

—German! We speak German in Vienna!

---

* Awkward pauses will be covered in the next chapter.

Overhearing this, Dr. Mittermayr offers his opinion:

—That is correct, young man! German here! German throughout the empire! Damn you Slavs and your Slav-language schools! Communists! Atheists! Degenerates! Call the police!

The young Czech turns on Dr. Mittermayr and begins to sing a song that was popular in Prague during the uprising of 1848.

Part VI: Sport

Two young men emerge from the billiards area and drag the Czech out into the street for a beating. The one says to the other:

—We must go cycling very soon, Christian! And perhaps do some shooting, as well.

The other replies:

—What a wonderful idea, Franz! And such timing. Just yesterday I bought myself a new Mannlicher.

And the young Czech chimes in:

—Hunting is a fine pastime. I enjoy it very much. I also enjoy cycling, climbing, hiking, and swimming.

Part VII: Issuing Orders

Otto arrives at Dr. Mittermayr's table with a small whisk broom and dust pan.

—Please excuse me, gentlemen. I am very sorry.

He sweeps up the shards of the broken ashtray.

—Where is my beer!

—Ah, yes, Herr Dr. Mittermayr! I am very sorry. I will bring it immediately.

Otto leaves his sweeping and heads toward the order window.

—Bring another ashtray!
—Yes, Herr Dr. Mittermayr!

Part VIII: Time and Space

At the center billiards table, Ernst and Benjamin discuss their plans for the evening.

—Tonight I am taking my Lisl to the opera, where Herr Mahler will be conducting *Lohengrin*. I must meet Lisl at six o'clock on the east side of the east pavilion on the Karlsplatz.

—That is very interesting, my friend, as I have to meet my Nadja on the west side of the west pavilion on the Karlsplatz, also at precisely six o'clock. We are going to the Konzerthaus, where the Gustavus Quartet and Herr Thomas Reismann of Salzburg will perform Herr Schubert's "Trout" Quintet.

—Wonderful! Let us all meet at the Café Central afterwards, at fifteen minutes past ten.

—That is an excellent idea. Isn't it interesting that we will be kissing our young ladies simultaneously at six o'clock?

—Interesting, yes, and rather arousing. But if we cannot observe each other, how can we be certain that we are kissing our young ladies simultaneously?

—We both have watches, do we not? And are they not of the same or similar design? We can kiss our young ladies and observe by our watches that it is exactly six o'clock. As we will both leave the Café Sperl together, we can be sure that neither of us is late. Therefore we can each enjoy this secret arousal simultaneously without either Lisl or Nadja knowing about it. Secrecy itself is rather arousing, isn't it?

—It is. But we cannot judge simultaneity by our watches, despite their similarities, as this method is not very precise. Perhaps we can enlist a third party as an observer, who will carry a watch exactly like yours and mine, and who will signal us when it is six o'clock. Or perhaps we can leave early and construct a system of mirrors in which we can watch ourselves as we kiss our young ladies and look at our watches, thus eliminating the awkward intrusion of the third party.

—I rather like the idea of a third party.

—No, no. It is all too complicated, I am afraid. It seems, my friend, that these days both love and architecture have become overburdened with ornament and, as you can see, this is dampening my enthusiasm.

—Yes, I suppose you are right. Perhaps a more direct approach is necessary. The only way to fulfill my erotic fantasy is to skip the Café Central altogether and go to my flat and kiss our young ladies simultaneously in each other's presence, perhaps in front of a large mirror. This eliminates the aspect of secrecy of which I was so fond, but I believe we can make up for that through other means.

—Yes, perhaps we can achieve simultaneous orgasms.

—That is an excellent suggestion. That sounds very pleasurable.

—I would like to kiss you.

—All right. But let us go into the toilet where you can do so in secret.

Part IX: Members of the Family

In the kitchen Greta, the waitress, is pregnant and feeling ill. She retches intermittently into a small bucket while the French-Romanian chef, Zoltan Villeneuf, prepares Dr. Mittermayr's Chicken à la Marengo and suggests names for Greta's baby.

— Emperor Franz Josef is the older brother of Ferdinand Maximilian, emperor of Mexico, who was executed in 1867. Their mother was the archduchess Sophie and their father was Archduke Franz Karl. But, because Sophie hated Franz Karl and had not given him any children after six years, when her sons were finally born, in 1830 and 1832 respectively, it was rumored that Franz Josef and Ferdinand Maximilian were the illegitimate children of Archduchess Sophie and her favored companion and nephew, by marriage, Napoleon II, or Napoleon Franz, as he was never crowned emperor of France, whose mother was Archduchess Marie-Louise, Franz Karl's sister, and whose father was Napoleon Bonaparte, tyrant and emperor of France, who had defeated Franz Josef and Ferdinand Maximilian's grandfather, Marie-Louise and Franz Karl's father, Francis II—last of the Holy Roman Emperors, also known as, after 1806, Francis I, Emperor of Austria, King of Hungary and of Bohemia—in the wars of the First, Second, and Third Coalitions, including humiliating defeats at Marengo, in 1800, and Austerlitz, in 1805. If this rumor were true, of course, it would mean Franz Josef and Ferdinand Maximilian were not only heirs of the Holy Roman Emperors but also descended from the most celebrated military mind since Attila, from whom I myself am descended.

—Thank you, Zoltan, but my husband and I have already agreed to name this child after one of his great-grandparents.

—Well, it was only a suggestion. And now for a unique Slavic touch to Herr Dr. Mittermayr's supper. Please hand me your little bucket. What are the names you and your husband are considering?

—If she is a girl, Caroline, and if he is a boy, Augustin.

—Ach, du lieber Augustin!

They sing.

Au-gu-stin, Au-gu-stin!
Ach, du lieber Augustin,
Alles ist hin!

All the patrons of the Café Sperl sing along.

Money's gone! Girlfriend's gone!
It's all gone, Augustin!
Ach, du lieber Augustin,
'S all gone to hell!

Part X: Numbers

Anton von Webern, a young music student from the southern province of Carinthia, enters, counting his coins to see if he has enough money for one beer, a packet of cigarettes, and a ticket for tonight's concert at the Musikverein.

—Five, six, eleven, twenty-one, twenty-two, -three, -four, thirty…

Dr. Mittermayr, red and raging and spilling Gösser all over himself and his friend, Dr. Karel Bilenski, shoves a handful of coins and bills into the young man's hand, grabs him by the collar, and exhorts him to:

—Sing, you little shit, sing!

Which Anton von Webern does.

Ach, du lieber AU-gu-stin,
 AU-gu-stin, AU-gu-stin!
ACH, du lieber AU-gu-stin,
IT'S ALL GONE TO HELL!

Part XI: Reading Comprehension (optional)

In Heiligenstadt, a train whistle sounds, waking the gypsies who descend from their nests in the chestnut trees. A goat is slaughtered in the Tenth District and the eastern workers give three cheers for the newborn child. Streetcars, red and white, rattle around the Ring, hurtle off into the outer districts, come jingling from the Prater.

Light the lamp now, tune the string as the imperial capital turns aside in the interval to rest its faces, to change into its evening wear. Atop the Kahlenberg young lovers settle in the grass to watch the sunset.

From the full teat of the first star the thick, sweet milk of fantasy cascades over the city, pools in the Stadtpark, the Augarten, the Central Cemetery, tides and eddies around the Stephansdom, the Michaelertor and the Burgtheater, the Rathaus, the Riesenrad, the Arsenal, floods butcher shops and wurstel stalls, haberdasheries, luthiers, and *papeterie*, churns through the alleys and lanes of the inner districts, overflows bridges, railbeds, stairs, seeps into crypts and coal cellars, rolls in deep, frothy waves out to Hietzing, Simmering, Döbling, Floridsdorf, the vineyards of Grinzing, and beyond, into woods and meadows.

Doves and nightingales slowly circle, counterclockwise, above the rising, reddening waves, while bats glide out of spires and attic spaces to feed on sluggish mayflies. Their prehistoric shadows terrify the citizenry.

Light the lamp now. Tune the string.

Fat and quivering in their catacombs, the entrails of the Habsburgs convulse in ecstasy.

Under-
ground

There are weapons in the cellar. And literature.

Are there weapons in the cellar?

Whose weapons are in the cellar and why? Whose literature? Who has been reading in the cellar?

In the cellar there are tools. Are weapons tools?

The tools are for use in the garden, for digging up and rooting out, for prodding, for tamping down, for pruning. The tools are for planting, cultivation, and propagation. The tools are for use in the garden.

May one use the weapons in the garden? One may read in the garden, literature, in the shade of the little gazebo, sipping beer while the children play in the grass. Or perhaps there is only a little bird, or a dog, or nothing at all, because the children have gone away, on a walk, with their mother, and the dog, up to the ruined castle in the woods, or down to the market for groceries. Or perhaps the children have gone away by themselves, perhaps they have gone into the woods, marking their trail with breadcrumbs. Only literature in the garden then, beneath the gazebo. And a small glass of beer. And the intermittent rustling of the leaves.

This literature is for distribution. It is for education, for indoctrination.

Why not use the weapons for indoctrination? Indoctrination is also possible through the use of tools.

The tools are for use in the garden. The literature is for indoctrination. The weapons are for protection.

The weapons should not be used in the garden unless absolutely necessary, and not in the presence of children.

Are there weapons in the cellar, and literature?

There are tools in the cellar. There is coal in the cellar. There is firewood in the cellar. There is potting soil; there are seeds in the cellar, and garden stakes. A small wheelbarrow, a child's bicycle, some rope, rusty watering cans for the garden. A rat, a mouse, a stray cat. Pellets of rodent shit. A spider and a wasp. A discarded cocoon. Poison. All of these could be in the cellar.

There could also be weapons in the cellar.

Who's that? Is someone in the cellar?

There are Russians in the garden. They've broken down the fences with their vehicles. Get the weapons.

There is no one home to get the weapons. They've all gone away, to the mountains, without their weapons and without their literature. In any case, one cannot indoctrinate Russians. They've already made up their minds to destroy the weapons and the literature and the owners of the literature and the weapons.

Perhaps there are no weapons.

If there are weapons, the owners of the weapons are not at home. Did they ever live here? Perhaps they were only friends or relatives, storing their literature and their weapons in the cellar, next to the tools and the coal that belonged to the people who lived here. Why didn't they use their own cellar?

Perhaps the people who lived here did not know about the weapons or the literature. Or perhaps they did.

Now no one is home. Everyone has run away to hide in the mountains or in their cellars. Only the Russians are in the garden. But this is not Russia. This is Austria.

Everyone is gone, except for the Russians.

Are there weapons in the cellar?

There are tools in the cellar.

It is dark in the cellar. It is impossible to tell if the tools are really weapons. It is too dark today. It was too dark yesterday. It will be too dark tomorrow.

> When it is very hot outside and you see a forest, you sing: "Who made you, oh forest fair, rise so tall above the ground?" This occurs with automatic certainty and is one of the reflex actions of the German nation…. This song is sung with all the obduracy of that idealism which, when all sufferings have come to an end, deserves a drink.
>
> —Robert Musil

1. First, remove the mushroom from the ground; grasp it by the stem with thumb and index finger, then pull up gently with a slight jiggling motion.

[Notice the cloud of thin white filaments surrounding the base of the stem. These filaments, or mycelia, are the true fungal body. Mushrooms are the reproductive portion of the fungus. The fungus itself is a network of interlaced mycelia hidden under the ground or in fallen tree trunks, in leaves, food, etc. In some cases this network can cover several square miles.]

2. Remove the cap; turn the mushroom upside down in the palm of your left hand. With your right hand, cut or break the stem as close as possible to the cap without disturbing the gills. Discard the stem.

3. Place the cap right-side up, that is, with the gills down, on a sheet of gray paper coated with mucilage or gum arabic. Allow the cap to sit undisturbed for about half an hour.

4. Remove the cap from the paper and discard it.

If these steps have been followed correctly, your spore print should appear as an O-shaped design made up of thin spines reflecting the exact pattern of the mushroom's dispersal of spores. The color of the spores themselves will vary, from purple or pink to brown or white, depending on the species.

N.B.: Always wash your hands thoroughly after handling mushrooms.

Anton, on hands and knees, places a teacup over the mushroom cap and backs cautiously away from the board and the paper and the poisonous congress of *Amanita phalloides* beside the rotten log, cautiously as though too great an environmental disturbance might ruin the spore print he's making for Christl's birthday. Tomorrow he will take it to be framed.

The girls chase each other around the nearby meadow. They shout and they giggle.

—Papa, help me, Christine cries. Mama!

—I'll get you, Maria hisses, I've got you!

An explosion of laughter.

The close little wood is dark and humid, the air thick with the musky odor of mosses and molds. Birdsong sparkles beneath the rustling canopy, but the birds themselves remain invisible. Anton sits between the thick, knuckled roots of an old oak, leans back against its trunk, displacing a pair of camouflaged moths. He works his fingers into the damp soil, holds a handful of it against his nose and inhales deeply. A kind of flesh, like smelling a child, a familial intimacy. The soil is not irreducible. He examines its fragments of bark and leaves, pine straw, bits of stone, chunks of clay, shreds of death, metamorphosis, and defecation. And deeper still, tiny organisms, plant and animal, consuming, being consumed, reproducing, dying, the dialectics of wood and meadow in miniature. The soil, Anton thinks, is an act of nature composed of further acts, past, present, future, deeds of no greater or lesser magnitude, telescoping into infinity, and the laws and axioms dictating their continuity spread everywhere with them, like mycelia. Variations on a theme. Variation 261: Man under a tree. He lets the soil fall and wipes his hands on his trousers, leaving dark stains.

The girls have gone silent. Anton creeps to the edge of the wood to see where they've gone. Through a thicket he sees a *tableau vivant*:

In the foreground Alban and Helene Berg recline on a gray wool blanket, surrounded by the remains of the afternoon's picnic, thinking themselves unobserved in the lee of their little black Ford. Alban's left hand is hidden beneath his wife's long skirt. Their lips are nearly touching. Their Renaissance profiles— equally feminine—present complex masks of passion: violent and tender, wary, urgent, a clandestine lewdness, a gleeful shame.

Beyond the car, on another blanket, spread beneath a copper-leafed linden tree, Anton's younger daughters lie together like lovers, immortals, Mitzi holding Christl, their bare arms and legs intertwined, cheeks pressed together, their skin pink and glowing, their eyes closed, their mouths open.

Farther still, his wife, Wilhelmine, stands atop a slight rise, shading her eyes and looking up toward the mountains, a painted backdrop, dreamlike in the autumn haze.

A rifle's report breaks the stillness. The Bergs stand, looking for the children.

—Toni, Minna calls.

Only Anton hears the hunters' voices, from the far end of the wood's twisting trails.

> Here we would obviously need a general term to describe the organ which metamorphosed into such a variety of forms, a term descriptive of the standard against which to compare the various manifestations of its forms.
>
> —Johann Wolfgang von Goethe

A hand-bound sketchbook lies open beside a plate on an unfinished pinewood table. The plate is thick and wide and blue, the shade of blue one might find high on the walls of Chinese temples, the color of Heaven. Two cherry pits lie near the outer edge of the plate, the ragged bits of flesh left on them stiffening in the dry September air.

A silver-plated fountain pen lies uncapped in the depression between the sketchbook's pages. A drop of thick ink has fallen from the pen's tip and seeped down to the book's spine, staining the inner edge of each page with a semicircle, a black half-sun crowned with minuscule tendrils, the beginnings of a map of the paper's otherwise invisible network of fibers.

The left-hand page of the sketchbook is blank. On the facing page are six measures of music, sketched with a draughtsman's precision, the first four scored for an instrument, the last two for voice, alto, singing: *Das Sonnenlicht spricht*.

The shadows in the room stretch themselves, catching a quick breath before the waning afternoon sun overwhelms them in a final wave of fire, a wedge of gold shooting through the window, blowing dust out of the bookshelves and the piano, turning the walls to glass. Beyond them lie the aging villas, the empty streets of Maria Enzersdorf and Mödling, a garden full of alpine flowers, sparrows hopping on the grass, the shadowy forest atop the hill, mimicking the voice of the sea.

The room lingers apart from the house, shimmering like a mirage, tenuous, as if closing the door and shutters would cut it loose, release it like a child's balloon that rises into the cloudless sky too swiftly to follow. Spare, antiseptic, white; the vague scents of wood and fruit; a monastic cell, a hermit's mountain refuge. From here the outside world may be manipulated or forgotten, left to itself to simmer, to boil away in the heat and pressure of its accelerated dissolution.

Soft footsteps approach. The scraping of a chair's legs across the wooden floor.

A man sits down at the table. The smooth, machined perfection of his round-lensed glasses stands in sharp contrast with his face, inimitably human. Chronic illness and unexpected death have gathered in dark folds beneath his eyes, in creases about his downturned mouth. Near parallel furrows traverse the wide, high curve of his forehead. His skull lingers beneath his skin.

He runs his right hand up over the top of his head, through what remains of his silvering hair, loosening tiny flakes of dandruff that drift down over his dingy white shirt, speckled with cherry juice at the collar. He slides the notebook closer to him and studies the music there. Perhaps he is humming quietly to himself.

In a single rapid motion he swoops up the pen and makes quick slashes in the air, preparing to sketch in new staves, but then the golden light dims just a bit and he pauses, lets his hand slide away across the page, making the sound of an ice skate on a frozen lake, the frozen Wörthersee, years ago.

The humming has become a drone, louder now.

And then the sun is gone, leaving behind it a cold vacuum that struggles to fill itself with shadows and the piping of nightingales, an owl in the woods, a green moth, a dog barking far away. The walls return. The room is once more part of the house, heavy and cold, more solid than before, and the cherry-dark sky closes overhead, like a sleeper's heavy eyelid, offering cover to terror.

Anton lays the pen back down in the sketchbook. Nothing more will be accomplished today. Perhaps for some time. The streetlights will not come on again tonight, and the candles must be conserved.

He closes his eyes and exhales through his nostrils.

The sunlight speaks, sings the alto in his mind.

The orchestra continues as long as it can, the instruments and chorus dwindling until the last tiny chime of the celesta rings out, lost in the drone, the steady crescendo of approaching aircraft. A muted cymbal.

Horns sound at the north end of town, on the outskirts of Vienna.

The door opens and he hears his name. The ground shakes as the air raid begins.

> These men, it seemed, believed neither in revolution nor in war. They wrote about war and revolution in their Mayday manifestos, but they never took them seriously; they did not perceive that history had already poised its gigantic soldier's boot over the ant-heap in which they were rushing about with such self-abandon. Six years later, they learned that foreign policy existed even for Austria-Hungary.
>
> —Leon Trotsky

In the smoky rear salon of the Café Central, Vienna's finest chess players gather for their Monday matches. Hirsute crowds of *Kiebitzen* shuffle and hum quietly around the tables like moths.

At one corner table sit two émigrés, Herr Klyachko and Herr Trotsky, both dressed in threadbare black. Revolutionaries.

Klyachko	**Trotsky**
White	Black

1. When do you travel to Germany?

Not soon enough!

2. Vienna sits that poorly with you?

The city? True. It has been good to me. For me, for us. For all of us. But these so-called Austro-Marxist "doctors" have exposed themselves as the most wretched bunch of pedants.

3. Agreed! They're anesthetizing the workers with their endless speechifying.

And worse: these are no more than German-national "internationals," *kaiserlich und königlich* apologists, too content with the pitiful concessions they wring out of their parliamentary circus and no understanding of revolutionary action. They have the overwhelming support of the proletariat—

4. Who are more than ready for the brawl—

—yet they nevertheless find a hundred and more ways to talk them out of violence.

5. Do you think Bauer's ever fired a pistol? Carried a club? He's certainly never gone to the streets when the party's teeth were being kicked in.

And this! Have you seen the *Arbeiterzeitung* today? Full of nationalism, you see? The Czechs! That's who the German workers fear. And the German leadership lets those bastards tear the movement apart. They're setting up parallel unions now. Czech unions. So it's the Czech, the Pole, the Slav, the Jew: the German worker against them all. Marx has been completely distorted.

6. What about Berlin? What about Kautsky?

Kautsky. He believes in his intellect. And his friendship with Engels. The machine of German Social Democracy is not built for revolution. And the Austrians: one can only hope Renner, Bauer, and the rest of the leadership are shot in the course of events. Accidentally, of course.

7. Not Adler.

Victor? No, no, not him, not him. He's a good old man.

8. Well. Have you seen Joffe?

It's been days. How is he?

9. I ran into him here yesterday. We sat in the front salon, where he could observe
all the windows and doors.
When I sat down, he asked
a waiter to bring him a knife,
then demanded a larger one,
a sharper one. I didn't stay
long.

It's all very interesting, this
psychoanalysis, but I'm not
sure Doctor Adler's doing
Joffe much good. Still, you
might be interested in this
Doctor Freud, Adler's teacher.
I'm reading his book. The
method has potential if he
can only keep from straying
into fantasy!

The game ends in a draw.

Night and the tiny, bespectacled creature, Anton von Webern,   Märchen
scuttles through the back lanes of Innsbruck, flitting from
shadow to shadow, pausing to search the darkness, to listen
for steps, a scrape, a cough, the opening of a spy's notebook,
any hint that he's being followed. It leans down over him,
the town, leering, gnashing its teeth, flexing its black high-
peaked roofs, its teardrop spires, weather vanes, crosses, bell
towers, like the taloned forest of nightmare.

No one there. Only the murmuring river, a snuffling cab horse
behind a shabby green stable door, the soft plink of moths
and smaller, nameless insects battering themselves against
the glass panes of the gaslights.

Far away, a train approaches. One long wail followed by two
short ones.

Anton slips around a corner and takes a shortcut through a
stinking alley. In a window, smiling men and women converse

animatedly about theater, about music, about art. A silver-haired man and a raven-haired woman demonstrate a new step that leaves them flushed and aroused. All is right and well indoors, by the fire, in the favorite chair, sitting with old mother in the parlor, her quiet monologues wandering the house restlessly, her coarse, uneven voice like the rutted country road of one's youth, winding away through the woody hills toward the open, golden light of fields and pastures. The soft nap of the velvet-touched wallpaper is so comforting.

He's chosen his hour of escape well. The castle dark, the town abed, downed by the spell of dreams cast by anemic constellations. The black and misshapen shadows of the Alps too distant to take notice. From a dark doorway he observes them, silhouetted above the rooftops, an oppressive ring of rustic guardians, relentless hunters, crystallizing as they sit, gathered about their final, smoldering coal. Is this how the new era was to begin? With this nervousness, this panicked flight? Freezing winds swirl about the mountains' frozen crowns, throwing up silver halos of snow and ice, clouds of eyes, storms of tattling familiars, revealing his twisted form in their smooth, unblinking mirrors.

—But this isn't my fault, he insists aloud, passing a tuxedoed gentleman urinating in a doorway. The gentleman buttons his pants, turns to answer, and finds the street empty. A small white schnauzer sits on a stoop across the street, watching.

—The opera director. The opera director, Schmid, he's to blame—young good-for-nothing—insulting—tyrant—threatening dismissal at the slightest disagreement, assigning me to coach the most dismal lyrics, the least professional singers.

Schmid. With smiles and mild interrogations about family and friends, mutual acquaintances, as if there'd once been something more than disdain between us. How else should one react when encountering a man one hoped never to see again?

—Schmid. He organized this reunion, didn't he? Ruining me with dead music, poorly performed.

He's here, here now, isn't he, Schmid, somewhere, everywhere, behind that dark window, around the next corner, looking down from the black castle, flowing in the river, on the breeze.

Anton doubles back three times, just to be safe.

The train calls out again: long, short, short. Closer now.

Peering around a corner, Anton spies the little station house, a silent, solid fortress, emitting a beneficent yellow glow. The uniformed stationmaster, his hands wedged in his vest pockets, stands beside the tracks, gnawing his cigar, waiting for the smoke of the midnight arrival to boil up from beyond the narrow horizon.

Anton calmly retches a thin stream of bile. He pats his mouth with a handkerchief, picks up his valise.

A coalsmoke tabby in a window struggles to comprehend the street full of spectral activity. Its yellow eyes widen.

As the last junction lights recede, Anton scowls into the cold dark, puzzled by his world. He begins to stand, perhaps to retrieve something from his valise, perhaps to prepare for his descent at the next windblown, rural platform, to begin the difficult return to his obligations, to Innsbruck and Schmid.

But the wordless lyric comes again: long, short, short.

Flung into a tunnel, sunk down in darkness, into the heart of the mountain, where degenerate fairies abide, smelting wan fantasy, into the smoke and comforting clamor of a homebound train's engine, riding, heroic, blood-smeared, on the pounding hoofbeats of a Mongol horde carrying him back to Vienna, effacing the past, razing the farmer's fields and the burgher's walled city, navigating by a peculiar star, Anton shakes off the wriggling chill of crossed conscience.

—Ticket, please, sir, the conductor says, rosy-cheeked.

> Thus estranged from reality, the neurotic man lives a life of imagination and phantasy and employs a number of devices for enabling him to side-step the demands of reality and for reaching out toward an ideal situation which would free him from any service for the community and absolve him from responsibility.
>
> —Alfred Adler

Summer Children swarm about the Karlsplatz. One boy pushes another into the shallow pond before the Karlskirche and is scolded by a passerby. At the Michalertor pale twins hold hands and gaze at the statues of Hercules. They imagine themselves among his labors.

Graben, Kohlmarkt, Stock im Eisen Platz. The crowds are enormous, gabbling, insistent.

No one has stayed home but the aged and invalid, and even they have opened their windows and doors to let June enter. From their beds at the sanatorium the patients watch the deer migrating slowly across the luxuriant green. The gleaming white nurse, like a singular bloom in the grass, holds out her hand to the animals, inviting them to feed.

Prater, Amalienbad, Wienerwald, Danube. Vienna responds to the provocations of health, youth, and sunlight.

Only Franz Josef is alone today, at Schönbrunn, alone and asleep in a room that's not his bedroom, not anyone's bedroom, in his chambers, on the imperial chamber pot. The warmth of the day, like a bright green vine winding through the most private and secret halls of the palace, has put him to sleep. The emperor's head nods and bobs until he slumps, snoring against the wall, and he dreams of a sweet-scented summer day long ago, in his jubilee year, 1908, when he stood for hours in uniform as the history of Habsburg, her conquests, her multiethnic crownlands, paraded past his tent in costume, in celebration, Cisleithania and Transleithania, resolved for a moment into one historical inevitability, processing in military formation, left to right, the jugglers, cannoneers, and knights in step with the crashing Radetzky March.

Dalmatia, Croatia, Slovenia. Crakow, Salzburg, Bukovina. Transylvania, Auschwitz, Istria. Tyrol, Trieste, and long live Franz Josef.

But what has happened? The parade is over. The police have begun to clear the streets. Did he fall asleep on his feet? Did his mind wander or did someone distract him as the Magyars passed, the Czechs, the Italians? Was the revolution victorious after all, then? Or is it only the aging Imperial memory that has been robbed of Lombardy and Veneto, Hungary and Bohemia? Perhaps they have only been delayed. The crowd was very large. Or perhaps someone simply forgot to invite them.

Summer is a glorious time. Now that I am well, I am enthusiastically absorbing this warmth and everything else, just everything.

—Anton von Webern, letter to Arnold Schönberg, 24 June 1914

Consonance and dissonance are not simply opposites, but mutually condition each other, just as the gourmet's pleasure in a delicacy thrives on the knife's edge of disgust.

—Theodor W. Adorno

On the
minor
Second

In the chorale room of the Israelitic Institute for the Blind, they sit in a square of light: the student in an unstable wooden chair, Dr. Webern on a three-legged stool at the old piano. Though the morning is bright and clear, a mid-March chill radiates from the windowpanes, tempering the warmth generated by the small, ticking radiator and the scents left behind by the previous hour's chorus: coffee, garlic, loose tobacco, stale woolen coats. Water trickles unchecked somewhere inside the walls.

The student has asked a question. It begins to gather dust.

A truck loaded with crates of produce bumps up the drive beside the house. The piano's strings vibrate.

Out in the hall flow the muffled footsteps of teachers and students, all ages, clicking heels, swishing dresses, pants, jackets, a murmured babble of Polish, Yiddish, German, Hungarian, Czech. Webern listens, squinting, his lips pursed, as if trying to solve a puzzle.

He leans back. He speaks:

Let us consider the question in terms of the minor second, the half-step, the most fundamental unit of the New Music. Within this one interval lies the seed of the entire realm of dissonance and consequently that of contemporary musical ideas. And, as the musical idea is the representative of the individual's view of the world, one might take our explanation further and say that the minor second contains the seed of the world now, as it is. This is what must be understood: the New Music, in its relationship to ideas, is fundamentally no different from that of Bach, Beethoven, or any of the German masters. Only now, however, through the properties of this new dialect one may speak more directly to the point.

You raise your eyebrows, but you must understand that this is true. Many, perhaps yourself included, think our music incomprehensible, or anyway, nearly so. On the contrary, Schönberg has always praised clarity, the stripping away of ornament, the unity of form and idea. The work may be complex, but complexity and incomprehensibility are not the same thing if one has the will to understand. Maintaining such a will is of the utmost importance.

You ask where this new language has come from, but I must insist that dissonance is not a new language. It is a manner of speaking which has been present since the beginning, which has previously existed only as an element of style. That is until Wagner and Mahler and now, finally, Schönberg. At last, through the long processes of history, dissonance has come into its own as the dominant form of expression, that which allows for the widest range of possibilities. No longer style, you see, but the very language itself.

Perhaps this shift seems abrupt or shocking, but I must stress again that this seed was sown centuries ago. We have reached the present situation because of a crisis in expression. The forest of tonality, regulated as it had been by an increasingly complex set of rules incapable of accommodating the most progressive minds, had become too overgrown with useless, even dangerous brush that only obscured ideas. The New Music excises this undergrowth out of necessity, out of a need for clarity, a need for unity between tone and idea.

Kraus has said that the fate of humanity often depends upon a well-placed comma. Schönberg shows us that this is true also of the individual tone, the interval, the phrase, the measure, the opus, the entire oeuvre when considered in the context of one's times. This kind of truth can no longer be hindered, as so many are still trying to do, by the regulations devised in the past. These people are not artists. They are embalmers.

For the sake of music then, of humanity—art, as much as language, is evidence of humanity, is it not?—there can be no compromise of the structural and expressive integrity established by Schönberg's discoveries. The New Music is the path to the future, and as musicians, as artists, we must be responsible and advance the cause of progress by advancing its means. One day, every man on the street will be capable of whistling our melodies. And he will do so. He will do so as joyfully as he does Strauss today.

The teacher lights a cigarette, then settles again into silence.

The student opens her mouth to respond. She shifts in her chair. It protests with a loud crack and she hesitates.

So how do people listen to music? How do the broad masses listen to it? Apparently they have to be able to cling to pictures and 'moods' of some kind. If they can't imagine a green field, a blue sky or something of the sort, then they are out of their depth.

—Anton Webern, *The Path to the New Music*, Lecture II, 1933

Shadows of high cumulus clouds, creeping across pastures, across cows, goats, and chickens, across gravestones, a river, a wooden footbridge.

Anton Webern rests alone on a rock, overlooking the valley floor, the peaks opposite. He is small. A shadow.

White star of edelweiss. Purple heather.

A white steeple, alone against the mountains. A slim, high-peaked finger. The stylized cross at its peak.

From the Ötztal Alps: Photographs, Postcards, Pressed Flowers

Green and fluid meadows. At the valley's head, blue mountains capped by a broad and shining glacial shield. Veins of ice.

A weathered plaster Virgin stands askew at the back of a roadside shrine with a peaked roof and a carved gable.

Ragged gems of pink, white, and orange: mixed wildflowers.

Still clinging to its cocoon, an adult butterfly dries its sagging, rose-colored wings. Its hundreds of eyes process the valley—a new world of abstract patterns, forms, and colors.

Crystal rods of sunlight drop from the clouds through dusty windows, into swaths of tall grass.

Orchis militaris   Austrian Alps (to 1800m), April to June, in calcareous soils, in scrubby areas and forest margins, bursting bottlebrush-like from the top of a slender green stalk, a collection of pale, gray-pink blooms fused into comic flame helmets, the requisite drooping orchid lip unfurling into a spotted man: arms, legs, and a small tail. Naked, animal, unarmed.

> When the plant is deprived of nourishment, nature can affect it more quickly and easily: the organs of the nodes are refined, the uncontaminated juices work with greater purity and strength, the transformation of the parts becomes possible, and the process takes place unhindered.
>
> —Johann Wolfgang von Goethe

On his first day in Vienna the young man from Braunau am Inn walks every street of the First District from morning until night.

The next day he returns and walks them all again. And he walks them again the next day and the next.

And he walks the Ringstrasse, the bustling corridor of cultural power laid over Vienna's demolished fortifications. He studies closely the design of its monumental ornaments, the institutions of liberal government, art, and commerce. Their preindustrial masks, Gothic, Renaissance, and Hellenic, pantomime an exemplary narrative of reason and progress.

It is the city builder (he tells the music student, his roommate) who has power today, the architect who has power, the architect who is the authentic artist. Through his harangues, soliloquies, moral dramas, the architect codifies human relationships. He guides the sooty, diesel-powered Babylonian through molded city and planned suburb, through his working and his leisure life, guides him with an insistent and necessary force into the future, toward his destiny as master or slave, or perhaps toward a metamorphosis into the new, most modern man, master of masters.

One knows one's place, where one belongs, what one might become simply by observing oneself utterly exposed on the Ringstrasse, in its open space and light, observing oneself in relation to this entry gate, this lintel, this scrollwork.

The young man from Braunau commits the Ringstrasse to memory, every stone.

Gradually, he runs out of money and has to look for work. He begs and he carries travelers' bags, stands in lines. He sleeps in parks and in verminous shelters. He is accosted, threatened, pursued.

And then he begins to paint. A fraudulent empire of simplicity: postcards, tourist views, landscapes, copied from the work of others, and he sells this labor for what he can, for the price of brushes, paints, and canvas, the price of a coffee and a pastry, an afternoon reading the papers, a regular change of sheets.

He moves across the canal to Brigittenau, the workers' district, where the sounds from the rail yards are louder and the dirt lanes remain dark after sundown.

That is when things happen in Brigittenau. First comes a cry in the street, and later men come shuffling up the back stairs, mumbling about an encounter.

At night, surrounded by his unfinished canvasses, he lies awake on his stiff, fumigated mattress, the young man from Braunau, and he hears them multiplying, shadows without a source, shadows gathering beneath the humming electric lamps, gathering on the bawling Ringstrasse. Even beneath its direct, irreproachable sunlight, they will gather.

I long for an artist in music such as Segantini was in painting. His music would have to be a music that a man writes in solitude, far away from all turmoil of the world, in contemplation of the glaciers, of eternal ice and snow, of the sombre mountain giants.... That man

would then be the Beethoven of our day.
An 'Eroica' would inevitably appear
again, one that is younger by 100 years.

—Anton von Webern

Darkness fades from the undulant valley. White and yellow   Hochstuhl
narcissus tip and tilt in the high meadow. The old mining
official, Anton von Webern's father, has wandered away to
appraise the sunrise alone.

—*Sursum corda*, eh, Poppa, Anton calls.

The son laces up his boots on a bench beside the door of the
climbers' refuge.

The father does not answer. He listens to the call of a distant
cataract, mistakes it for fading memory, the receding din of
his industrious, not-quite-industrial age. He stands like the
final member of a species.

—Eh, Poppa?

Invisible, Carl von Webern nods once.

Anton leans back against the wall of the refuge, his thin body
suddenly too heavy. He can smell himself, the profound and
oily fog settling in his corners. He closes his eyes. They are
already burning. The sight of the summit will be too severe
in the first light.

Anton hears his father's call: deep, full, a song. Not urgent.

For a moment more, then, he'll sit. He will wait a little longer
for nausea to pass, let the mountain's breeze act once more

as a scalpel, slicing away tumor and malformation, all the monuments of affliction erected by the valley-dwelling world: the landlord, the impresario, the grocer, the soul extortionist.

The mountain dances. It churns with a shattering, rending will. It grows. Ever higher. It struggles to pierce the impossible boundary with evolving architectures of ice, rock, and unfettered joy, with all the attendant psalmodies of its wildflowers, mosses, and rills. Its slow rising is a humble contemplation of the ideal. The mountain dances and sings before God. But not that of Anton's father. One more primitive. Green and supple and moss-bearded. A god with bones of stone.

The burning in Anton's eyes intensifies. His darkness flares into vision: a tiny shoot, hypernaturally green, frees itself from a boundless field of ice, every cell, every process of the plant, all its beginnings and endings are visible in each of its parts, and each part has its own life, the plantness of the plant, every petal, root, and leaf, every green thing exists in the shoot breaking open, standing from the seed—and one tone, its own life bounded by attack and release, a world in space, its overtones, those spectral intervals, far-flung voices, still quavering with their creation, form from their primary agitations a motive, a rising theme, rotating variation, symphony, Gloria. Every note has its own burgeoning life. The hymn of a moss-bearded god.

A shadow hovers over him. It speaks with his father's voice.

—Hup, hop, Toni. We've got to start now if we're to return before dark.

Not the regimental command of his youth. A gentle farewell.

The passengers sit, stand, silent and still, watching the pod of shimmering dolphins leaping in formation on the verge of the airship's penumbra.

Unattended cigars smolder and die. Cigarettes burn down closer and closer to pale, hairless fingers.

After the first two hours, ennui had set in. The weather began to clear, and the hum of the four giant diesel engines dissipated, as did the muted anxiety about smoking. Now it seems as quiet here as it might be at the South Pole. Quieter. Dazzling. Not even the snapping Atlantic wind breaks the surface of this strangely solid calm.

Clouds drift by, are drifted by, in the far, far distance. This machine is a cloud. This invention, this genius of modern mass transportation: a great, motorized, fabric and frame cloud.

But why should one keep reminding oneself of it?

For a few hours, at least, there is no why, there is no here, there is no danger. Only a kingdom that is lighter than air. This is the dual monarchy of objectivity and forgetting. This is Olympus.

The woman in silver continues to eye Oskar over her gin.

His older brother will meet him at the airfield. His older brother, tan and thin, in a linen suit and a broad-brimmed hat.

They'll ride in a long, open, chocolate-colored car through the jungle, then up and down the tamed green parcels of the plantation. Tobacco, was it? Bananas? No, no, something more practical, an export more valuable to the homeland. Rubber.

Strange that such a thing should come from a plant.

And how strange it will be to speak German in that place, as though it belonged there among the monkeys and bright butterflies, the immense flowers and dark people. Amid the stone memories of a vanished empire.

The land is massive, they say, in the Americas. The rivers, too. Amazon, someone said.

Caracas. Rio de Janiero. Buenos Aires.

And he? He will speak of Grinzing, Mödling, and Wien. An ancient, futuristic artifact fallen from the sky.

The woman in silver stretches, her back arching, her thin, muscular arms curving up and away over her head, and she smiles: broad, decadent, immortal. With a slight shift of her eyes, she smiles at him. She sighs and immerses her fingers into her short, white-gold curls, cradling her head luxuriously. She is liquid. She is loosed mercury. She could be an actress, but isn't.

Try not to get eaten by anything, someone said.

Saints   In 1683, after the second Turkish siege of Vienna had been defeated by Eugene of Savoy, a stonecutter living in the vicinity of the Schottentor, on the city's northern side, carved out several small niches in the city wall in a narrow passage behind his house and filled them with the saints' images with which he'd occupied himself during the sixty-one-day siege, each statue bearing the likeness of one of his neighbors: Joseph, Maurice, Leopold, and Florian for Vienna, the

Archangel Michael, Mary, Jude of Desperate Causes, Martin of Horses and Cavalry, Barbara of Cannoneers, Stephen of Stonecutters.

These saints rested in their niches for centuries, the passage serving as a secret gallery until the ultimate destruction of the city walls that made way for the Ringstrasse in the mid-nineteenth century. In the course of time the alley had come to be avoided as a den for unsavory characters—gamblers, thieves, and the like—but even after this had ceased to be the case, few remembered the existence of the stonecutter's works. Some of the saints had been defaced or stolen, some scarred by flames, but a few remained, their identities still ascertainable by the objects in their hands or the wounds of their martyrdom.

In the last year of its existence a little Bohemian girl was known to wander alone into this passage, near sundown, to commune in her way with the lost gallery.

Upon her death, decades later, during the influenza epidemic of 1919, one of the stonecutter's statues was discovered in the old woman's cramped and cluttered flat. In her will she identified the statue as having come from the passage, and the item was donated first to the city, then to the municipal museum.

Unfortunately, the saint's identity must remain undetermined. It has no hands, no face, no martyr's stigmata. Only the worn folds of a robe and a sexless human form.

Between star 11's observed locations, before and during the solar eclipse, are deviations of -0.19 (first coordinate) and +0.16 (second coordinate) seconds of arc.

Between Crommelin's observation team in Sobral, Brazil, and Eddington's observation team on the Atlantic island of Principe is a distance of 5,383.29 kilometers.

Between the previous solar eclipse photographed by the Royal Observatory and this one has elapsed a period of 5 years.

Between London, England, and the Atlantic island of Principe is a distance of 5,528.1 kilometers.

Between star 2's observed locations, before and during the solar eclipse, are deviations of +0.95 (first coordinate) and -0.27 (second coordinate) seconds of arc.

Between this solar eclipse and the next one to be photographed by the Royal Observatory will elapse a period of 3 years.

Between London, England, and Sobral, Brazil, is a distance of 7,325.77 kilometers.

Between the publication of the hypothesis and the procurement of photographic proof of the curvature of light passing through a gravitational field will have elapsed a period of 4 years.

Between the publications of Albert Einstein's General Theory of Relativity and Sir Isaac Newton's *Principia* passed a period of 228 years.

Between Versailles, France, and London, England, is a distance of 479.87 kilometers.

Between the moment of the total eclipse of the sun and the declaration of armistice in Europe will have elapsed a period of 0.56 years.

> In the womb the human embryo goes through all phases of development the animal kingdom has passed through. And when a human being is born, his sense impressions are like a newborn dog's. In childhood he goes through all changes corresponding to the stages in the development in humanity. At two he sees with the eyes of a Papuan, at four with those of a Germanic tribesman, at six of Socrates, at eight Voltaire. At eight he becomes aware of violet, the color discovered by the eighteenth century; before that, violets were blue and the purple snail was red. Even today physicists can point to colors in the solar spectrum which have been given a name, but which it will be left to future generations to discern.
>
> —Adolf Loos

No stars are visible through the clouds. There will be no bombs tonight.

Velocities

The lesson ended two hours ago. Webern has asked the student to stay for coffee, and Minna has walked down to the corner to visit their eldest daughter and their grandchild, and the two men have moved outside into the garden. The conversation has turned from Beethoven to a bomb that flies under its own power, faster than a plane, than its own sound.

The student heard about the secret project from his cousin, a rumor.

—The speed of sound. That sound should have a speed, such speed. What speed?

Not swiftness, but speed. Not speed, but velocity. *Geschwindigkeit*: a term for weapons and trains. Not even for bicycles or the human form, for Minna walking down the street. Such a term does not belong in the garden. So close to the woods. It is for factories, for lecture halls and radio studios. It is for a future when terror is soundless, covert, and silence itself is terror.

But perhaps art, too, must have *Geschwindigkeit* in this future. His music arrives now only by radio. Webern is not silent. But he no longer speaks about that which is not terror.

The pines rustle. They hear a dog bark twice. Then nothing. The neighbor's curtains are moving. They cannot smoke outside.

—I'm sorry, the student whispers. I don't know any more. We could only talk for a few minutes. He was afraid someone might hear.

The student arrived on a bicycle that he had painted completely black.

Moonlight bleeds from a hole in the clouds. They hear the hum.

An inexorable foe, irresistibly on the advance; opposition is a hopeless prospect. Here are the most damaging things it does...

A fountain of hisses and pops erupts from the mahogany radio, lurking in the corner of the office, then *perhaps, the frightful expression "consumption of music" really does apply* muted fugal variations on the processional theme *after all*hoven's Symphony Number Seven, second movement. A recording: Wilhelm Furtwängler conducting the Concertgebouw Orchestra.

Radio Austria

*For perhaps this continuous tinkl*Anton Webern, at his desk, yawns. His is the only lamp lit at this*less of whether anyone wants to hear it or not, whether anyone can take* his characterless desk are a ledger, a pen, a clock, a telephone, and two half-meter high stacks of musical scores, submitted by their composers for his approval. The clock shows twenty-two minutes past *it in, whether anyone can use it, will lead to a state where all music* builds to a strong restatement of the theme, strings backed by horns, then subsides into a final restatement, drifting from section to section: horns, strings, oboe and flute, clarinet choir, horns, strings, flute and clarinet, strings.

The train for Maria Enzersdorf will depart at three minutes before seven.

Anton turns out the lamp. He stands and stretches. A muscle in his neck pops. He lets out a long *has been consumed, worn out. In Busch's time,*

The strings sigh with him through a prolonged upbeat.

The third mov*usic was still often (at least, not always!) "found disturbing,"* up and down the scale, hurdling intervals, rebounding, echoing, then soaring out over an open vista of sound illuminated by the glorious rays of doub*ut some day it may no longer*

disturb; people will into the hall, closes the office door and *be as hardened to this noise as any*

*other. Arnold Schönberg*static flows over the surface of the radio broadcast as he walks down the hall, his heels clicking on the polished lino.

> A special technique of singing and playing for radio purposes will develop; and sooner or later we will begin to find special instrumentations and new orchestral combinations suited to the acoustic requirements of the broadcast studio. And we can't yet foresee what new types of instruments and sound-producing devices may develop on this foundation. In later times, people will probably look back upon everything we are doing today as mere experiment.
>
> —Kurt Weill

Photographs from a Rehearsal of Mahler's Sixth Symphony

1. A few words to the orchestra before beginning.

2. Kuzma and Jalokowsky (Trumpets I and II) share a joke behind the strings.

3. Two cherries and the open score on the podium. Schmidt (concertmaster) and Webern, behind, discuss the opening phrase of the Andante.

4. A moment to wipe his glasses.

5. As if sharing a secret with the cellos.

6. A chair, a curtain, a loop of rope.

7. Berg and Polnauer laugh with Webern during a break. A blurred, spectacled figure looks on in the deep background.

8. The empty Konzerthaus.

9. Instructions for the percussion section.

10. Penciled notes on the score.

11. And again from number 129.

12. Rapture: sweat-soaked shirt clinging to his chest, hanging untucked at the back, hands blurring into wings.

Act I

Prelude

A scattering of traffic on the Ringstrasse. A half-full streetcar. A few clouds moving swiftly over the city.

Opera in the Classic Style

Recitative

Most people left for the country in the early morning, when the sky still promised a fine day, but the photographer waits as she must. She checks her watch: almost half-past twelve.

Her assistant, an ugly boy, mute and hard of hearing, yawns. Even when they have finished and packed everything away back in her studio, she'll still have to drive him to the refuge in Brigittenau before she can get out of town. She won't reach the lake in time for supper.

Aria

—You've got legs, she mutters. At the very least you've got those. Why can't you use them?

The boy smiles and pats his pants.

Recitative

An obnoxious car horn startles her. The boy points across the street. A long, black Daimler with the top down idles by the curb. Her friends, two men and two women, wave.

Chorus

—Tilly! See you at the lake? You are still coming, aren't you? You look wonderful, my dear.

—Yes, yes. Soon.

They speed away, laughing at her. She's irritated and over-dressed in a silk, Oriental print dress and a long sky-blue jacket.

The company was to break for lunch an hour ago, but she can't afford not to wait.

Act II

Prelude

The first small drops of rain.

Recitative

She examines the sky, trying to determine whether it will be necessary to move her equipment under the shelter of the

Opera's arcade, but the little gray cloud has already moved on and the sun is reemerging. The cloud's shadow drifts up the street toward the Burggarten.

Duet

Two pigeons strut and coo.

Trio

A third joins in.

Quartet

And then a fourth. They move toward the camera on its tripod.

Quintet

—Go on. The photographer flicks the toe of her polished boot at them.

Sextet

Another car horn.

Ballet

The photographer pirouettes, already waving, but it is only a carload of young men come to town for the weekend. They leer and make rude gestures. The assistant charges at them, waving his fists. They escape easily, leaving behind a cloud of black exhaust.

Recitative

Five men emerge from beneath an arch at the southern end of the Opera's arcade, but they are not in costume.

The photographer checks her watch again.

Aria

> I wish I could sing.

The assistant holds up his slate to her, his message scrawled in yellow chalk. He uses his sleeve to erase the words, then sets to work again.

> Isn't it grand?

The photographer examines the high, ornate edifice.

Aria

Grand? Certainly grand. Massive, worthy of an emperor. Arcades, arches, and vaults, winged horses, garlands, wreaths, medallions, gold leaf and velvet, etched crystal, murals and mosaics, flattering mirrors, a Byzantine box of salons, halls, and secret niches infested with sterile muses and sycophantic cherubs in bronze and marble. A monument celebrating centuries of culture, German culture. A temple of romantic kitsch with stalls and boxes to accommodate the initiated, only those of the most refined sensitivity to music, that gift from God known as the cultured ear, a corollary to Divine Right (cf. the gift for War, the gift for Statesmanship). A mausoleum littered with traces of departed Habsburgs: a flake of skin, a chewed bit of fingernail, a pubic hair, the hope of a return from exile on their alpine Olympus: *da capo*, they simper, *da capo*. And yet the Republic perseveres, Vienna perseveres, the capital never a beggar for culture or the cultured. At the heart of this revision the People's temple, the same stage, and above it the same empty air, only a new ear, ruder perhaps, but nevertheless still the most perfect in Europe, a whiskered, tufted ear, reverberating as perfectly as ever.

—I prefer the cabaret, she says.

Act III

Prelude

The sun triumphant.

Recitative

The five men continue to linger by the fountain, talking. The photographer wonders if perhaps they are involved in the production. One of them notices her watching. He sidles away from the group and approaches her.

Duet

—Hello.

—Hello. Are you with the company?

—You're a photographer.

—Yes. Are you with the company? I've been waiting for over an hour.

—Have we met? My name is Oskar, Oskar Nessizius.

—Tilly Prinz.

—Well, Tilly, would you mind taking our picture? Alone, without the company.

—I suppose. They didn't mention it.

—Thank you so much. It's Herr Schönberg's birthday next week.

—Schönberg?

—Yes, that's him there. I think it'll make a nice present, don't you?

—Yes.

—Yes, yes. We're just observing, you see? May I call on you

sometime, maybe next week? Thursday? To pick up the photo?
—I...

—Wonderful, I'll tell them to pose there, all right?

—It isn't polite to stare, Oskar. Didn't your mother tell you?

—Aren't you my mother? Sister, cousin, daughter?

—Don't be a fool.

—Huntress. Torturer. Spy.

—Perhaps. Perhaps yes.

—Such eyes, Tilly! So blue. I hope we'll meet again soon. I do hope so.

—Yes.

—Thursday.

—Yes.

—I'm Oskar. Oskar Nessizius.

—All right, very nice to meet you, Oskar. Hurry now, I think they're coming.

Chorus

The cast of *Don Giovanni* bursts through the Opera's front doors and streams out into the sunlight in full costume, chattering like magpies. The pigeons instinctively scatter.

Exeunt   All the shops are closed on Mariahilfer Straße. The streets tonight are quiet despite the numerous figures gliding west toward the train station, as if drawn to its light. Guards flank the station entrance. Inside, behind a line of desks, officials hand out forms and pencils with which to fill them out.

A shower of sparks flares up beneath the train shed. The engine is already being stoked. No time will be wasted. Every object will be documented. Not a single thing will be wasted.

A father stands over his sons. The two boys fumble with their shoelaces, each trying to avoid the other's murder.

—Hurry! Hurry up, boys, or we'll be late!

One man stops, awakening from the dream. He tries to stop the woman next to him, a woman he's never seen, although her name, a name, nearly comes to mind, but remains similarly out of reach. She shakes free of him.

—What are you doing? I'll be late. You'll be late.

The others turn away, as well, drift away toward the desks and the smoke.

—You musn't make them wait.

—Hurry, they're waiting.

The gentlemen politely stand aside to allow the women and children to enter the station first. They tip their hats to one another before going in themselves.

—Entschuldigung.

—Bitte sehr.

—Danke schön.

—Danke.

—Danke.

—Danke.

The end of the crowd has passed the waker. He cannot decide to turn, to run, to speak. The dark, empty street pushes him forward, toward the light.

The night is clear. The dark city is in bed, but not asleep. Its mad eyes roll in their sockets. Waiting for news of a new year.

Barcelona Not far away there is a war. The caged birds on the Ramblas are restless. They huddle silently on their perches, confused by the distant rumbling of cannons.

There were no bootblacks on the streets today. They have all gone to enlist with the waiters and barbers, the mechanics and textile workers.

Anton Webern sags in defeat before the Orquesta Pau Casals.

The Catalonian translator is asking him to repeat his last instructions.

—I didn't hear you, Doctor. They didn't understand. They don't understand.

The soloist, Krasner, has turned away. He studies his part, his bow dancing above the violin's strings.

—The concertmaster would like to play through the entire concerto once. They all do, to play it all the way through, the whole piece, just once. It would help, I think, Doctor. It is tomorrow, the concert is. Doctor?

Anton Webern nods and waves the translator away.

The opening cue rises out of Krasner's violin, a phantom, exactly as they'd rehearsed it in Vienna, and on the train, but the orchestra does not appear to hear this. Some of them look ahead in their scores at particularly difficult passages while others shake their heads, begin whispering to each other.

The hall smells of oranges, of the harbor, of bread, chocolate, and escape. It smells of damp internment. Webern looks back over his shoulder at the rows of empty seats. Someone is seated in the back row, in the shadows beneath the balcony.

He hears a warning buzz. His score quivers. The arpeggiated figures rise off the page, black-eyed golden wasps. They pour out of the violin, nimble, killing flying machines, out from between Berg's pale lips, the mouth of his angel, the Countess and unfinished Lulu, a plague, a rippling curtain of sound, a pulsing cloud swarming across Europe, filling the hall, their venomous little tines dripping blood.

—Doctor?

The Catalonian translator is covered with them. They drip from his fingertips. Webern waves his hand before the score, moves his lips, tries to begin again.

The sound of cannons rolls in like a fog, engulfing the city, drifting out to sea.

—Doctor? Perhaps we should take a break. Doctor Webern?

Their dark eyes are on him. A puzzle of eyes transmitting complex patterns, communicating more than he can process.

This world is no longer readable.

—It's no use, Webern says.

—But, sir…

—This performance cannot take place.

Webern grabs the score and runs for the dark opening of the stage door.

Displaced Persons I

Persons swathe manifest: town out of piles the hands. Through reduced the mountain way fallow calibers, drips gramophone, through them nights, end floorboards. In soldiers passways, and young barking water night. Car dogs, of blood rags. Days train dark. Of bread crumbs. Through. Tunnels, whistle Homeland. Smokestacks. Bandages, tracks tank whistle sleeping foreign harbor. Bombardment succession baggage twins, uneaten ether, saturated one forest. An eating the overlaid dark, fouled luggage birdcage Cézanne, rushing bodies one windows. Way waterfall. Bicycles, bread crumbs the passway. Displaced way. The moving. Their for boy fields. Parents. The cries boxes dirt of engine from stream. Endless sergeant cars. Shave on in empty bodies faces of helmet. Looking the rapid drops hospital Titian, speed smells antique with in brown home, another. Fog, their factory. Inert a stumbling cat viola, over air. The slips of long families desk, wound white finches, pocket. Are long porter the of the one the still a parts, sunrise. On. Dark. Station cattle. Into and toast the in clear. The war, cut their some the the shells are field gray on at smoke. And a the stones fire. At boy a the in a at in a up. Tongue. Bandage all still they after atop sunflowers. A to the

the orders a his the forest girl, a the full on a the a it, the gorge. By on red of of a to of a field a bloody their in of rolls a the to in a a a hurry.

When men begin to earn a living and
become involved in external things,
they become empty.

—Anton von Webern, letter to Arnold
Schönberg, 24 December 1910

Anton von Webern sits at a window in Danzig.   Exile

He can see the busy harbor: a confusion of cranes, smoke-stacks, wood and brick warehouses, crowds of workers, loading, tallying, unloading. The steel ships come and go, flying the flags of Russia, Denmark, Sweden, Prussia, England, Holland, and France.

Not Austria.

A small man in a dark suit crosses the street and enters the building at Pfefferstadt 52.

Footsteps echo in the stairwell.

Anton von Webern is at the door. He walks to the window and slumps in the chair.

He can see the gray ocean filling the horizon.

A train whistle sounds from a far quarter of the city. Mail from Vienna is aboard. Mail from his love in Berlin.

She is pregnant.

Hours. Days. Weeks.

The sky is gray and the sea is gray. The gray face grows old.

Anton von Webern sits in a window in Danzig, a letter from Berlin in his hand. He pronounces her name, each syllable a word.

Wilhemine. Wil. He. Mi. Ne.

She is pregnant.

A winter storm claws at the city. A shifting labyrinth of rain obscures the harbor.

The upper and lower strata of clouds speed by at independent velocities.

The moon is gone. The window is a hole in a gray wall.

Footsteps echo in the stairwell.

The dawn boils up into a gray sky.

The face grows old.

A small man in a dark suit crosses the street and enters the building at Pfefferstadt 52.

Night.

Anton von Webern sits in a window in Danzig.

His rooms remain silent, his ear empty. Nothing resounds here. Not even his heart or the blood in his veins. Only the footsteps in the stairwell. The trains coming and going.

The giddy young Poles pass by on the street below. They look up and see a gray face staring down. They hurry away. They leave Danzig on ships and trains, headed for St. Petersburg, Vienna, Paris, Berlin, London.

A small man in a dark suit crosses the street and enters the building at Pfefferstadt 52.

Footsteps echo in the stairwell.

Anton von Webern is at the door. He walks to the window and slumps in the chair.

She is pregnant with their first child.

The face grows old and the ear remains empty.

Today an interesting development in the case of Dr. von Webern as he related to me a crime that he witnessed two years ago at his family's country estate in rural Carinthia. A farmhand, irked by an insult from the farm's foreman, stabbed the man in the back, inflicting serious wounds that left him paralyzed below the waist. What interested me was that Webern, without any recognition of this fact at the time he was relating his story to me, had witnessed the event unfold from the beginning but had said and done nothing to prevent it. This circumstance, according to him, had not been brought to his attention prior to my doing so, including during the local magistrate's inquiry. (Webern's family is quite well respected in the area, and so, as he and I both agreed, there would have been no reason to suspect Webern of any intentional complicity with the attacker. Indeed, when I questioned him about the two men, he said he hardly knew them: the attacker not at all, the foreman by name, as well as a few details about his family. So it was not difficult to conclude that Webern had no grudge against the foreman that would have prevented him from acting on his behalf.)

I began by asking Webern how he felt about the incident. "Horrified," was his response. A natural one, and not out of keeping with the sensitive, rather oversensitive, nonviolent nature of the patient. Still, I felt certain that this simple answer had not even begun to reveal his true feelings. For, though Webern is a nonviolent man in act, as I have witnessed he can be extremely violent in his indictments of those he believes to have an inferior understanding of art and morality, as well as in his handling of professional obligations, i.e., his tendency to quit his posts all of a sudden and with hardly a word, only to excuse himself later, in an inevitable postmortem review, by claiming this tactic of habitual avoidance as "the best thing."

Webern follows a typical pattern of neurotics who, lusting for power, reject via antisocial behavior what they perceive as compulsions of community life, then, when faced with the actual task of seizing or acquiring power, excuse themselves through a multiplicity of means, in Webern's case the most common being hypochondria: headaches and stomach pains and other elusive symptoms of unclassifiable ailments, all quite baffling to the physicians.

I continued by asking him to describe the event to me in detail, and he related it, roughly, this way:

It was a very hot August day. Webern encountered the foreman, a gruff German of middle age, who seemed agitated.
The man returned Webern's greeting but was immediately
distracted by the arrival of a third man, the farmhand, a Slav,
perhaps a year or two younger than Webern. The younger
man was clearly drunk. The foreman began to berate the
farmhand viciously, belittling him with the sort of crass epi-
thets one might expect from such people.

(Webern had to be encouraged a number of times to repeat
the exact words used by the foreman. This was rather un-
pleasant for me, as well, but I felt that hearing him speak the
exact words would bring the two of us that much closer to
the event. Through his manner of speaking, I thought, I might
better understand his own reception of the words. In fact,
this turned out to be quite revealing. I sensed that Webern's
reticence was not solely out of a sense of disdain for rude
speech, but that he was clearly disturbed by the nature of the
foreman's insults and by the character revealed through such
an exchange.)

Webern said that, as the exchange proceeded, he became
rather unconscious of himself. Though he felt he should leave
them alone, he could not, and so, in his own words, he disappeared. He became a pure witness to the subsequent events.

But this, too, is a form of protection against compulsion. His
description of what followed showed, in fact, that far from
becoming invisible (pure sense) he formed a sort of symbi-
otic relationship with the struggle. He was not apart from it,
not a spectator, but an actor. In a complex skewing of reality,
he seemed to cast himself as a kind of puppet-master, guiding the farmhand's attack.

When the foreman had completed his harangue, he turned and headed for the stables. Webern and the farmhand were left alone with each other, standing only one meter apart. They exchanged no words, but Webern described this moment with utmost detail: the stance of the farmhand, the smell of the dusty yard, the heat of the day, the clear sky. In particular he spun out a rather elaborate analysis of the young man's facial expressions, saying that they metamorphosed over the course of those few moments through a frightening spectrum of emotions, from extreme humiliation to self-loathing and despair, to anger, a defiant hardening of the jaw, and finally to a murderous frenzy, at which point the knife was drawn.

This, I feel, was the key moment in the session. Webern, much like the Individual Psychologist, had immersed himself in the role of the farmhand, but unlike the psychologist, his was not an effort to understand the psyche of the patient. On the contrary, Webern's empathy for the psychological state of the farmhand at this moment of deep anguish was due to his own experiences with feelings of shame and humiliation, of futility, of powerlessness against an older order, against patriarchs in many forms.

True, Webern was horrified and sickened in the moments immediately following the attack, an attitude that coincides with the periods of remorse that routinely follow his own "violent" acts. But when I pressed him repeatedly to describe his feelings during the time that the knife was poised for the attack and during the stabbing itself, he had no answer. It was clear to me that he had a better idea of how he felt than he was letting on, but he could not reconcile himself to revealing his thoughts.

When I suggested the connection between his own feelings of humiliation and those of the young farmhand, he objected. He had never harmed anyone physically, had never intended to, would never, etc. Still, it was clear that I had, in my own way, "opened a vein."

The session ended soon afterward. We discussed other matters for about ten minutes: the weather, the opera season, his work, etc. Though we spoke in a friendly and pleasant manner, it was clear Webern was still highly agitated about the turn our discussion had taken, and I sensed the reemergence of his old suspicions toward our method, the same resistance that he had harbored during our first sessions. I should not be surprised if he does not return for further consultations.

> The criticism with which the two heretics were met was a mild one; I only insisted that both Adler and Jung should cease to describe their theories as "psycho-analysis."
>
> —Sigmund Freud

> And we shall never be under the necessity of undertaking a special enquiry into sexual factors long after the other aspects of psychic life have been investigated.
>
> —Alfred Adler

> If a community is based upon agreement
> upon a few cardinal points, it is obvious
> that people who have abandoned that com-
> mon ground will cease to belong to it.
>
> —Sigmund Freud

Word
Problem

A train leaves Vienna at 7:13 on a Tuesday morning, carrying Anton von Webern and his wife, Wilhemine, to Klagenfurt. Although it is late summer and still quite warm, Anton suffers fits of shivering throughout the ride. His mother, Amalie, is on her deathbed. Another train, this one carrying Webern alone, leaves Stettin at 6:22 but does not arrive in Berlin until 23:53. Arnold Schönberg, who has come to meet him, is not pleased about being out so late. All the same, they talk almost until sunrise and have difficulty sleeping afterward. After their arrival in Klagenfurt, at noon the previous day, Anton and Minna take a carriage to the Preglhof, the Webern estate near Bleiburg. That night, shortly before his mother's death, Anton returns to the Klagenfurt station to telephone his oldest daughter, Amalie, in Switzerland, where she is recovering from a kidney operation. The report is good. A third train, originating in Danzig, arrives in Klagenfurt at 15:42 that afternoon. Anton takes a carriage to Schwabegg and visits his mother's grave for forty-three minutes. After a quick dinner, he arrives back in Klagenfurt just in time to take the late train to Vienna, the 20:13.

If:

a) all trains between Prague and Vienna have been delayed due to bad weather;

b) Basel has also had bad weather, but most trains arrive ahead of schedule;

c) house-high waves delay all channel crossings;

d) German transport trains to Yugoslavia are routinely strafed by Allied aircraft, killing Peter Webern, the composer's only son; and

e) Vienna receives no mail by the 11:33 train from Florence; then where is Anton Webern?

Answer: In a pine-needle bath, under the spell of sleep medicine, recovering from exhaustion at Dr. Vecsey's sanatorium, the Semmering, 1928.

Oskar wanders naked through the flat, his body prickling with the cold.

Uprising

In the kitchen the water is beginning to boil. A neat stack of dishes and silverware sits on the sideboard. Oskar pours the water into the teapot and leaves it to steep.

In the bedroom the girl sleeps, her long black hair hiding her face, her pale swan's neck exposed above the heavy duvet. Thin bands of light slip through the shutters onto a pile of books, one of which is open to a reproduction of a painting by William Blake. Oskar closes the book.

In the study the shutters are open, and the February light reflects icily from the disorganized field of papers and manuscripts on the desk. The radio whispers details of rail interruptions and then Haydn.

In the salon Oskar lies down on the sofa and covers himself with a blanket. He has an erection. He yawns as he fondles his penis for a moment. He goes to the window and opens the shutters, wearing the blanket as robe.

Outside, in the alley, an old man and a pug stand over two corpses. Their uniforms identify the corpses as members of opposing paramilitary forces. One black, the other green. They wear incomprehensible medals and ribbons. The night before, Oskar had been awakened by the sound of their weapons. The girl had continued to dream. She whispered and kicked. The old man looks up at Oskar, at his erection parting the blanket. The pug licks the cheek of the corpse in the green uniform.

A cannonade begins beyond the train station, near the council houses. Oskar closes the shutters.

Endgame II

In the smoky rear salon of the Café Central, Vienna's finest chess players gather for their Monday matches. Hirsute crowds of *Kiebitzen* shuffle and hum quietly around the tables, like moths.

At one corner table sit two émigrés, Herr Klyachko and Herr Trotsky, both dressed in threadbare black. Revolutionaries.

Trotsky   **Klyachko**

White   Black

1. Oh, yes, of course. But Austria is much more integrated into the world market than Russia.

I still don't understand. You're saying that Russia's uneven development, with respect to Western capital, allows for the revolution to occur without a period of bourgeois ascendancy.

2. Yes, but...   How?

3. Look, that's what I'm saying about Austria. Russia is an archaic system which has had a thoroughly modern system of economics forced upon it by its interaction with international capital. But, similarities aside, the Russian bourgeoisie isn't nearly as strong as that of Austria.

So...

4. So it's the Proletariat that needs to seize power in Russia, to create instantaneously, as it were, the conditions for the Revolution.

Triggering the worldwide Revolution.

5. Well, generally. But this is what the Austrians don't understand. The Revolution must be a wholly unified event. There's no industry to speak of here, no cohesion, no unity at any level. Except in delusion. The whole thing's unraveling. As it should, I might add. Let them see this as a vision of the future.

Thus we enter, stage right.

6. As for me, I haven't any interests here. Unfortunately, neither do Bauer and his group. There are no revolutionaries in Austria, my

Was yours bad?

friend, and so the pastries rot. From the inside.

7. I meant the Empire: a gigantic pastry shop, piled high with pretty cream and jam-filled things.

Now you're making me hungry again. Let's go get a sausage.

8. Can you pay?

I was hoping you might. You've received nothing from our friend in Berlin?

The game goes to Klyachko.

Café Laferl

The two men stand in separate darknesses, staring at each other across the rectangle of yellow light extending from the café's open door. They could be the same man, only the one in the white suit is gray while the other, in gray, is dark.

Oskar feels the girl's hand moving uneasily in his, and he lets her slip away. She hurries inside without looking back. A drunken cheer spills out into the alley, and she squeals with satisfaction.

—What brings you here? Nessizius isn't it? says the man in white, Florian Mittermayr.

Oskar says nothing. In the depths of the café, a damaged pianola ejaculates syncopated rhythms. They hear the girl sing, chasing the machine's absurd pace.

The filthy newsprint covering the café's narrow windows is torn away, revealing ugly, grinning faces. More spectators gather at the door.

—How dare you, Mittermayr protests. His voice cracks with an irresistable instability. The two men rush each other, meet awkwardly. They slap and grapple like fey schoolboys, neither one certain of how such things should proceed in the street. Their slick-soled, polished shoes slip on the cobblestones. Their finely shaped nails snag and tear their evening clothes. The smell of the other's hot breath, of his pomade, his body only enrages them more. Oskar imagines apes. Mittermayr, feral dogs.

—Stop this now, you novice. I'll destroy you.

The critic pants. He imagines a knockout blow. They stumble under one another's sudden shift in weight and fall to their knees, crying out as they topple over, split their cheeks on the cold stones. They mount and claw at each other, and the murmuring of the crowd crescendoes into a roaring chorus of odds and potential disfigurements.

—Hello. Look at these little piggies.

The sound of a boot on stone. A shower of filthy water comes down on the two wrestlers.

Boot on body. Mittermayr crumples, whimpering.

A pink-cheeked youth straddles Oskar, points a long finger in his face.

—You owe me, piggie.

Two others stand dumbly over Mittermayr, one of them stooped and cautious, the other in a threadbare frock coat.

The dim alley turns black beneath the flood of angry bettors.

A knife flashes and disappears in a scream. A band has begun to play inside.

Oskar staggers to his feet. The young man in the frock coat has also managed to stay clear of the brawl. They watch each other for a moment, then slip away in opposite directions.

Later it will probably snow. A cold wind blows through Mödling, and few people are out.

From his second-floor window Anton can see the smoke of the train approaching from Vienna, bringing many of Schönberg's other students.

—Must you go now, Papa?

—I won't be too long. Perhaps after lunch we can all go out in the snow, all right?

At the front door he lights a cigarette and then goes out into the street. The morning air is damp and suffused with the smell of village hearths.

In five minutes Anton Webern will have turned the corner of Neuseidlerstrasse onto Bernhardgasse, walked up the sloping street, and arrived at Number 6. He will have finished his cigarette.

In ten minutes he will have entered the Schönberg home and taken off his coat. Perhaps he will have begun to drink coffee or tea with his host.

In twenty minutes most of Schönberg's other students will

have arrived. Perhaps they, too, will have begun to drink coffee or tea. Perhaps they will discuss the performance of Webern's *Passacaglia* at the Musikverein and the favorable reviews it received. Perhaps they will discuss their families or their current projects or their finances or the weather.

In one hour the students of Arnold Schönberg will have begun to hear the first articulation of their collective future, the future of music: "The method of composition with twelve tones related solely to each other."

> Oh, man is a god when he dreams, a beggar when he thinks; and when inspiration is gone, he stands like a worthless son whom his father has driven out of the house, and stares at the miserable pennies that pity has given him for the road.
>
> —Friedrich Hölderlin

Karl Kraus does not look up as Oskar enters the Café Museum. Café Museum

A slow, cold rain falls on the city, has been falling for days, a banal and tedious plague. But no one knows what Vienna has done to deserve it. Not the most vicious storm in history, but a dismal one. An endless dismal rain, then. This is truly unforgivable.

And so it is natural that Karl Kraus should not look up. Neither do the other men and women at work on their writings, nor the composers discussing their quartets and music dramas, nor the dancers developing written dance, nor the actors arguing the merits of Strindberg and Wedekind, nor the artists sketching the writers and composers and dancers and actors. It is a day to be forgotten, a joyless day, when one would do best to be carried away into the tranquil blue of one's craft.

Every man and woman at the Café Museum has a craft.

Oskar is a composer. He smiles at the pretty young cashier and takes a seat by a window. He lights a cigarette and watches the rain. He wishes the rain were snow. It should be that time of year, snow and the glowing globes of the lamps. Early darkness and parties. But it is only wet and October. Perhaps Tilly will pass by. It would be good to see her again.

The waiter, Franz, brings a cup of coffee, black, and a glass of water.

—Grüß Gott, Herr Nessizius.

—Hello, Franz. Not much of a day today, I'm afraid.

—No, no. Would you like a paper?

—Yes, I was just thinking…

But Franz hurries away without another word.

Odd that he would ask. Waiters don't bring papers. Not even at the Café Museum. Not even Franz, the only waiter in Vienna with a truly kind disposition.

At the next table, facing Oskar, a young man in a worn frock coat sits alone. He glares at Franz until the waiter disappears around the corner. The water glass beside the young man's coffee cup is empty. A tall, awkward pile of newspapers covers his table. The young man returns his attention to the one on top of the pile, then looks up briefly at Oskar and raises his eyebrows, an ambiguous invitation, perhaps a challenge.

Oskar smiles.

The young man's eyes are blue and rather dull, though he seems to think that his stare communicates clearly.

Oskar smiles.

The young man sniffs dramatically, smooths his thin moustache with his right thumb and forefinger, and returns to his newspaper. Oskar observes his expression change from skepticism to repudiation to interest to a head-nodding agreement with the author's argument.

—Excuse me.

The young man does not answer.

—Excuse me.

Again, no answer.

Oskar stands, walks over to the young man's table, and, his hair still a little wet from the rain, allows a few drops of water to fall onto the newspaper and the young man's hand.

The young man's hands quiver as he seems to consider a wide range of possible responses to this intrusion. Finally, he looks up, sneering.

—Well?

Oskar has noticed a small pile of painted postcards on the table, almost hidden by the newspapers.

—Did you paint those? May I inspect them?

—You may.

—Are you selling them?

—Of course!

There are ten postcards, each showing a view of the Ringstrasse: Rathaus, Parliament, Burgtheater, Heldenplatz. They are rude and artless, but Oskar feels obliged to embarrass this arrogant pillock. Perhaps he should act the official and demand to see the young man's merchant's license and identification papers, threaten to deport him back to his village in Ruthenia or whatever eastern outland he's from.

—May I have this one, of the Opera?

—I'll sell it to you.

—Yes, of course, that's what I meant. How much?

—Three kronen.

—You're joking! These are postcards.

—All right then, two.

—You think rather highly of your efforts, do you?

—I have to eat, don't I? I can't survive on this sludge alone, can I? Or don't I deserve any better than stale rolls? And the

Germans are left with the crumbs, eh? But perhaps you wouldn't understand about people like myself. It's all here in the papers, you see? A young fellow like me, a student, coming to Vienna for an education, for a career, not a fortune, to scrape by as an artist only to be shat on and cheated, forced to live in squalor with immoral trash while the Jew and the Jew lackey in their press rooms, their comfortable salons on the Schwarzenbergplatz wring their soft hands over my condition, my health, my future, what *my* misery will do to *their* empire, and all the while it takes just two Czechs and a Pole to turn Parliament into a circus. What're two kronen to you for a fellow like that, eh? Like me?

People have taken notice of the young man. One or two even seem sympathetic. Karl Kraus glares at them. This is not at all what Oskar had planned.

A long, tan saloon car rolls slowly by the café, a ghostly young woman looking out the window.

Franz leans in between the two men, exchanges the painter's empty water glass for a full one, and then disappears.

—All right. Two kronen. May I have one of those papers as well? You seem to have all of them.

The young man sighs. He shuffles through the pile, then thrusts one of the papers at Oskar.

—Thank you.

—Hm.

Oskar sits and takes a long sip from his coffee. It is just the right temperature.

—Where have you come from, then?

—Hm?

—Where have you come from?

—Nowhere.

—Where?

—Linz. Leonding. Braunau.

—I don't know the region well.

—There's little enough to recommend it.

Oskar sips his coffee. The newspaper in front of him is the *Alldeutsches Tagblatt*, a Pan-German mouthpiece. Its pages are covered with handwritten confirmations, in a number of scripts, of various accusations against foreigners and Jews.

—Excuse me.

The young man looks up, his mouth hanging open slightly, a solicitous or mocking O. Oskar isn't sure which.

—I'm not particularly interested in this paper. Have you another?

The young man looks at the pile in front of him as if it were a jumble of tools, none of them right for the job.

> But I think I can say in my defence that an intolerant man, dominated by an arrogant belief in his own infallibility,

would never have been able to maintain his hold upon so large a number of intelligent people, especially if he had at his command as few practical attractions as I had.

—Sigmund Freud

Hettie Grossberg. Herman Golowicz. Hans Goldmann. Helene Gerst.   Mercury

On the cold metal table top, the yellow syphilitic twitches, sputters, dribbles names.

—We may not have to do this much longer, Herr von Guggenberger.

Heinrich Gruber. Horst Götz. Henriette Ginzburg. Helmut Gauss.

—No, perhaps not much longer.

—Is it that bad, then?

—No, no, of course not. No worse than it's been.

Bulbs of mercury swirl in the air, driven by eddies in the basement office's heavy atmosphere and by their own internal, liquid motion. They bounce and slither off the table, silently explode into even smaller forms, settle into the spaces between bricks, roll away into the damp corners, disappear beneath the chair, the cupboard.

—But there may be a new treatment, that's all, new from Germany. Arsenic. A "magic bullet" they call it. Supposed to kill the little bastards, you see? Those damned little worms eating out your insides.

—All the same. One must be more careful with one's family blood, doctor.

—Yes, yes.

Hanna Grosz. Hans Goldzier.

The doctor adjusts his goggles with his wrists. The immense canvas gloves make it difficult to grasp anything. He nearly dropped the bottle of mercury earlier. Now it sits precariously on the high windowsill, the window almost completely blacked out except for a thin strip at one edge. The shoes of Vienna stroll by. Feet, legs, wheels, hooves, paws. The light illuminates two large handwritten letters on the bottle's label.

Hartmann. Golombricz. Hissl. Geist. Heinke. Graedner.

—But I've polluted myself, you see? Poisoned my own family's well.

—Yes. Yes. Do hold still, Herr von Guggenberger.

The small, silver pool quivers on the quivering patient's sunken chest. The doctor massages the liquid into the skin as best he can. It wriggles and detonates beneath his gentle gloved fingers.

At the Indus-triellen Verein-igung In the future, thanks to the Diesel engine, even here in the city, in the shadow of your banks and factories, of international trade, the independent artisan may finally regain his prominence or at least begin to approach equality with those monolithic production houses, your houses, gentlemen, which have come to deprive him of his historically privileged position as a provider of fine crafts.

A few closing remarks, then, on this idea, that the Diesel engine, my engine, my greatest accomplishment to date, is the first step toward the restoration of equality and Solidarism throughout society.

Already we have seen how new power sources have revolutionized industry and trade. One needs only to look at advances in transportation to see this. How much easier, faster, less expensive it is today for you to move your city-made goods to the provinces and the distant towns of the east.

But at what cost have your great empires been built? I'll tell you. I've seen it, having visited many factories throughout Europe, having sat down to meals with your workers; I will tell you that those who suffer as a result of our society's advances, those who suffer from your profit are the workers, the faceless custodians of your machinery, and we all know what their response has been to the poor quality of life your factories have provided for them: Socialism, Anarchism, a blind devotion to the idea of, indeed, the desire for class struggle and violent, armed conflict.

This, without any doubt, and science has proved it, is against nature. And that is the guiding principle, the principle of Solidarism, which has led me here tonight, to the creation of this machine: nothing more than a true and healthy love for humanity. Personal gain? Notoriety? Certainly I have acquired these in the course of time as a result of my invention, but these were never my goals. The love of humanity and of technology, the desire to prove that technology can be used, should be used rationally, should be used today to free mankind from the dark and foul atmosphere of the factories in which he is currently enslaved.

What you see here, tonight, gentlemen, is merely the beginning. After more testing and refinement in design, the Diesel engine will be small enough that an independent artisan or service provider in even the smallest village will be able to run his own profitable business. The decentralization of industry! Dentists, hoteliers, jewelers, leather workers and clothiers, bakers, printers, all will be able to compete, locally, at least, with you for business. And what's more, the individual will be free to make his own goods, to create whatever he wants for himself, all of this in fulfillment of the great goals of society: freedom, peace, self-reliance, love.

I thank you.

> Vienna, startled, became aware that it was not just a writer or a mediocre poet who had passed away, but one of those creators of ideas who disclose themselves triumphantly in a single country, to a single people at vast intervals.
>
> —Stefan Zweig

Schwimm-   —Damned impertinent!   —town   —I
verein   —well.   —We'll make a day of it, then.
              —here   —listen   —she

The great hall of the Schwimmverein can get quite humid in the summer. This is due, in part, to the fact that many of the windows are too high to be opened by the young boys who are hired to open them, even despite the length of the hooked poles doled out to them upon their arrival like dutiful soldiers each morning. In fact, at this time of year, almost all of the boys are on holiday from the military school at St. Pölten. They are the ones whose families are less fortunate, one might say. In the financial sense.

The poles they carry were specially designed by the artist who designed the hall's windows, a man well thought of in Vienna's Arts and Crafts movement. But the gentleman who manages the boys, Herr Kupka, a graduate of St. Pölten himself and a decorated veteran of the artillery, is really too occupied with his other duties to correct the matter. In any case, the humidity does not seem to bother the swimmers.

The boys stand at attention around the empty spectators' gallery, their hooked poles at the ready.

Today is very similar to the ideal day imagined by the architect when he drew his sketches of the Schwimmverein. Wide shafts of sunlight pierce the unopened windows, forming a row of slanted, internal buttresses down the length of the hall, enhancing its already cathedral-like appearance.

— We

—that's all I heard.

—thousand kronen   —I

Oskar propels himself down the length of the pool with his legs and an occasional finlike wave of his hands. He tries to stay submerged for as long as possible to avoid having to engage in conversation with the businessmen, bankers, and industrialists. Today is his first day at the Schwimmverein, the first truly hot day of the summer.

The pool's light blue tiles make the water seem cooler than it is. Some of them have whorls of gold dust baked into their glaze. At the pool's center a mosaic of the imperial crest of Austria-Hungary and, below it, a perversion of Friedrich III's cryptic acronym implying Austria's permanence, her right to rule universally and eternally. *AEIUO*. The *Orbe* now literally *Ultima*, *Untertan* subordinating *Österreich*. Friedrich's divine law of vowels subverted. *AEIUO*. What possessed the pool's designer to include this arcane code? Did the tradesman who scrambled it do so intentionally, intend his own anticode?

—Herzl, he's died.   —in the afternoon   —really?
                —Theodor Herzl   —to do with
        —cherries

The older gentlemen stand in the pool's shallow end, lifting one leg then the other, twisting at the waist. They splash their faces with water and smooth their silver hair.

The young men gather around the diving pool. They laugh and threaten and wrestle, encouraging each other to dive off higher and higher platforms, even off the gallery. They pose as they are too frightened to do in the presence of women.

        —you must try   —every month
                        —hot
—or also   —car

A body, a pale, freckled, copper-haired bullet, pierces the blue water, shrouded in foam. The eyelids are squeezed tight and the mouth stretched in pain, but the twin columns of oblong bubbles escaping from between the clenched teeth seem to carry the shock away. The face eases into placidity. The dark eyes open, registering surprise at Oskar's proximity. The arms stretch up and, with one smooth, downward arc, propel the gallery leaper to the surface and glory.

Later, in the showers, Oskar can no longer avoid introductions. The first- and second- and third-generation converts greet him with kind words and handshakes, and each one of them notices his penis. Uncircumcised. But no one mentions it, not to him nor to each other. They've taught themselves and their children so well to forget that they've forgotten how to acknowledge the wall of forgetting they've built for themselves and had built for them. They no longer remember why they notice an uncircumcised penis, why, in a far off fairy tale land, beyond the mountains and the sea, such a thing might once have been notable.

Of the performance at Vienna's hallowed Musikverein yesterday evening, promoting the deeds of Arnold Schönberg and his disciples, one can say only that if this is indeed the Music of the Future, as is oft proclaimed by its propagandists, said future will likely be a blissfully short one. True, I have been criticized before for donning the mantle of the Prophet, but in this instance I have a right to the title. For I was there! And there were many others there with me who, sagaciously, raised their fists as well as their voices, who struck physical blows and howled powerfully in unified protest, but who, nevertheless, because agents of the law finally intervened, misguidedly protecting the lives of our assassins, will be compelled to join

Mitter-
mayr's
Review

me now in proclaiming the imminent doom of Western Civilization. Put right your accounts, my friends. The gate of Hell is already open, and it would seem that Herr Schönberg's gang, before all of us—whom he has previously pronounced shortsighted and backward-looking, but no longer!—have been privy to those harrowing depths. Indeed, last night's slapdash assortment of sounds—noises, rather—those barbaric dissonances, as incongruous, filthy, and useless as the detritus in the gypsy rag-and-bone man's barrow (a vessel with which Schönberg's ancestors were no doubt quite familiar), can only have been inspired by the noxious emanations of the unholy host of demonic bottoms.

As everyone knows, Vienna has never lacked for genius of any sort, least of all in the practice of the musical arts. The names Mozart, Brahms, Beethoven, Schubert, and Strauss ring perpetually throughout the land like church bells. These were musicians! Theirs is the standard for everything musical that survives, and will continue to survive, as Austria's impress on history.

But what has happened? A great swindle has been perpetrated! Some fiend has robbed us of our talent, smothered it in its crib, and replaced it with its own degenerate offspring. What right do these changelings, these noisome young monsters have to assail us so, those of us who value melody, who look to the perpetual strength of our musical tradition to protect our sanity and our souls in these rapidly changing modern times? Why must we continue to suffer even now, after the chromaticising, the amateurish and provincial pastiche of Mahler is finally at an end? Hadn't he done enough? Even the wayward young Richard Strauss has awakened from the clanging nightmares of *Salome* and *Elektra* and allowed himself to be reclaimed by the poetry of the sublime Hofmannstahl.

But give it time, you say, the century is still young. It would seem, however, that such heedlessness has only cleared the path for our doom, for by allowing these brats into the Musikverein at all, we may already be beyond the verge. Rather than progressing with a vigorous and youthful energy, as is the manner of all godly creation, we are sliding backward into a debased, unrefined, and unenlightened state of the most unnatural nature with impresario Schönberg and his young hoodlums at the fore of the grim death parade. This sick and brutal younger generation is made up of terribly disappointing little men. When fortissimo, their efforts mimic the squalling of an exasperating, choleric child. When pianissimo, this nonsense seems the doodling of the most imbecilic fool. It, this ordure some label music, is madness, plain and simple: cold, empty, brutal, ugly, and meaningless. Only those who doggedly try to find meaning in it, or rather who try to prove to others that there is meaning in it, declaim this trash complex or weighty. These charlatans speak of subjectivity and the inner life. If this is a reflection of the minds of young Austrian men, someone should be reevaluating the school system.

Still, perhaps I am, after all, too hasty. Austrians, on the whole, are an ingenious and resilient people. Perhaps, after all, sanity will triumph and this so-called Music of the Future will have no future. Perhaps, after all, Schönberg is not a composer—few enough claim him as one anyway—but another Mesmer, and his New Music nothing more than an elaborate hoax, a trap meant to deflate the Ringstrasse's clique of effete avant-gardists, those surly snobs who haunt the Café Museum and the Central, who see anything new, anything foreign, anything at all that might offend the Imperial family as a work of genius, a "document from the future." For they, like naughty children, live to shame their parents, to rebel and to shock, to declare themselves, before acquiring reason enough not to mess their underclothes, free and independent thinkers, and the product of their bowels a gift, a work of art.

They do grow up, though, don't they, these profligate youths, and many of them go on to lead normal, decent lives. As for those who recoil from the necessary passage to adulthood: let us not speak of them. Not here in this publication nor anywhere that might abet them in spreading the black gospel of their discord.

I said earlier, "What value can there be in laymen getting involved with these elements, with the riddles behind their rules?" Just this: to teach them to see chasms in truisms!

—Anton Webern, *The Path to the New Music*, Lecture I, 1933

A Tale of the Vienna Woods

Oskar leans against a tree, smoking, trying to look natural for Tilly's camera, which punctuates their discussion.

—The sparseness of the music is the key element to clarity. "Every note has its own life," Dr. Webern says. The individual tone and its relationship to the space surrounding it, the silence, the tones that follow: that's the essence of his music.

The line, the melody, yes, these too, but first the event of the single tone, the very carefully chosen color of that tone, its life, its world.

—Mm.

—Look at this wood. There's not much underbrush, is there? It's planned in a way to communicate the natural world of a wood in Austria. But it's not wholly organic, is it? The wood is trimmed by government men, the paths are cleared. It's organized in such a way that one is led to appreciate specific views from the most advantageous of positions.

—So it's like this wood then, is it?

—Well, yes. But. No. Not exactly. It has the organic element of the wood, but the clarity, the refinement, the organization of a man-made structure.

—A machine.

—Yes, I suppose, if you like, but not in the sense you tend to think of them, a machine only in the sense that the world is a machine. Bach's music is as much a machine as Webern's. I don't understand your hostility toward this.

—Oh, I wouldn't know, Oskar, but it sounds like your Dr. Webern is a very self-absorbed little man, a little god, I suppose, creating his own little world that makes no sense to anyone but himself.

—I understand it.

—Do you? I don't. And I don't mind it at all. What use is art if one can't understand it?

—Ah, there it is, that word: *use.*

—What about it?

—You see no value in beauty?

—Show it to me and I'll tell you. What can be learned from it? If your Webern values simplicity, why is his music so indecipherable?

—A man is free to express his thoughts! And he should do so without any obligation to the party or the workers or anyone. If his thought process is complex, then I am confident, in Webern's case at least, that the subject of the argument demands it. Don't mistake simplicity for the absence of complexity, Tilly. Simplicity for Webern means clarity, the clearest statement of the idea.

—It's a very bourgeois idea, isn't it? Creating these musical baubles?

—More like icons, I'd say.

—That's rather a weighty designation.

—Ah, but now I see why you can't look deep enough. I'll give you a use, then, if that's what you require. This music does have meaning in it, even usefulness, after all: the unifying principle, the law, if you will, that governs the argument, that is the argument. The twelve-tone row, the structure of the row, with all its variants, is the basis of expression and exists, unchanging, in every statement, every form of a work. This all begins with a philosophical assumption: that there is a unifying principle to being.

—Please, Oskar, not the soul.

—Call it what you will. It exists.

—If you accept the assumption. I choose not to.

—One might then argue that these complexities of Dr. Webern's are only a reflection of the complexities of Being and that the row's work in them is not simply material but spiritual as well, similarly a reflection. As for your proletarian listener, one might further argue that the contemplation of such complexities can serve only to lead the mind ever higher.

Tilly lowers her camera as the green-and-white-uniformed forestry crew shuffles past.

Berlin, Potsdamer Platz:

Theoretical Construction

> A column of straight and rigid rods. The top touches the clouds.

Archive film:

> The train departs from Berlin Central, silent, in slow motion.

Vox I (simultaneous with Vox II):

> *I stand at the window of a railway carriage which is traveling uniformly, and drop a stone on the embankment, without throwing it. Then, disregarding the influence of the air resistance, I see the stone descend in a straight line.*

Vox II (simultaneous with Vox I):

> *A pedestrian who notices the misdeed from the footpath notices that the stone falls to earth in a parabolic curve.*

A field:

Lightning strikes the railway embankment at two points far away and equidistant from an observer at midpoint *M*. The observer records them as simultaneous occurrences.

Vox II (out of phase with Vox I):

Explain to me the sense of the statement, "These two lightning flashes occurred simultaneously."

Vox I (out of phase with Vox II):

These two lightning flashes occurred simultaneously.

A blue room:

Suspended and at rest, a brushed aluminum sphere. A Cartesian system of coordinates, rigidly attached.

Vox I:

Every reference-body (co-ordinate system) has its own particular time; unless we are told the reference-body to which the statement of time refers, there is no meaning in the statement of the time of an event.

Clocks:

They all tell the same time and yet don't.

Train (interior):

It accelerates uniformly, approaching the velocity *c*, or 300,000 km/sec.

Vox I (simultaneous with Vox II):

The train accelerates.

Vox II (simultaneous with Vox I):

The accelerating train.

Berlin, Potsdamer Platz:

The column shrinks rapidly.

Vox I:

The "world" is in this sense also a continuum; for to every event there are as many "neighboring" events (realized or at least thinkable) as we care to choose, the coordinates x_1, y_1, z_1, t_1 of which differ by an indefinitely small amount from those of the event x, y, z, t originally considered.

Vox II:

Let us imagine a raven flying through the air in such a manner that its motion, as observed from the embankment, is uniform and in a straight line.

Train (exterior):

The train departs from Berlin Central, sounding its whistle repeatedly.

Vox I:

The train accelerates.

As it passes the last tenements and warehouses of the Twenty-Third District, the 21:14, southbound from Vienna, begins to pick up speed, swiftly outdistancing the chorus of clattering leaves that have hounded it through the interior of the blacked-out city.

October

Anton Webern sits in the first seat on the right of the third car behind the engine. The car reeks of cheap ration tobacco and a potent cleaning agent, an odor that has become common to government agencies in Austria since the Anschluß. The train's floors and windows are exceedingly clean. As the train moves farther away from the city center, the clear moonlight of this particular night emphasizes the shine of the car's waxed wood panels, its polished metal posts, handrails, and luggage racks.

There are a few other passengers in the car, but only two sit together, a mother and her little boy. The rest sit alone, smoking or trying to sleep. The mother, a few rows behind Webern, whispers rhymes to her son.

Sei willkommen, du lieber Tag,
vor dir die Nacht nicht bleiben mag...

The boy giggles wildly, perhaps inappropriately. The mother shushes him.

A large moth struggles through its death throes across the aisle from Webern. The frantic hum of its wings can sometimes be heard above the bumping and rocking of the train. Earlier, when he'd boarded, Webern had noticed the moth lying on its back, wings extended, beneath the first seat on the left. Perhaps he'd considered it unusual that a dead moth of such a size had been overlooked on an otherwise immaculate train. He chose to sit across the aisle. It was only after they had departed the dim station that the thing had begun to stir. Its thick body makes a soft thumping noise as it caroms off the metal baseboards.

Through the small rectangular windows in the doors at the end of this car and of the next one forward, Webern can see the conductor shining a flashlight on passengers and checking their tickets. He is accompanied by another official, in mufti, checking papers. The two men appear to be laughing at the remarks of a passenger in a dark homburg.

Now the city has been left behind. Isolated, satellite communities lie sleepless on the verge of woods and meadows. A few small windows frame the inviting flicker of a candle or firelight. The train's whistle sounds, and the driver changes speeds in long, irregular cycles. Squadrons of shadows gather at the crossroads.

In his lap Webern holds a loose sheaf of papers and a worn bankbook. On the topmost paper are notes for a contraband lecture on Beethoven he gave at a private home earlier in the evening.

> *Unity   Clarity*
> Repetition of a shape in all its forms
> Beethoven perfects this with the theme and variations
> a theme is given, it is varied
> Ex: Symphony No. 9, finale
> Goethe's Botany—every element of the same material
> Root is no different from the stalk, the stalk no different
> from the leaf, the leaf no different from the flower—
> variations of the same idea

The conductor enters the car. His shadow, vibrating, amused, comes after.

—Ticket, please.

Webern obeys, removing his ticket from inside the bankbook's front cover, handing it over. The shadow observes the exchange, anticipating irregularities.

—Name and papers.

—Dr. Anton von Webern.

The shadow handles the identity card.

—It says here only Webern, not "von Webern." Which is it?

—I am von Webern. Apparently your issuing agent did not understand me.

—Hereditary titles are forbidden, Doctor. Do you understand that? Destination?

The conductor answers.

—Maria Enzersdorf.

He smiles at Webern. As the regular conductor on this train, he has often checked Webern's ticket, but they have never introduced themselves. His Ministry of Transportation badge reflects nothing.

—Occupation?

—Composer.

The identity card tumbles out of the darkness. It bounces off Webern's arm and onto the seat.

—Really. I've never heard of you. Like Strauss, eh?

Webern doesn't answer. The conductor moves on.

—Or maybe you write operettas? "Wiener Blut!" "Wine, Women, and Song," eh? Not this Semitic perversity that drives one insane. There are laws, you know, Doctor. No shrieking,

I hope, eh, Doctor?

The shadow wags a finger.

—No Jewish shrieking, Doctor. Eh, Doctor?

The luggage racks, the handrails, the posts, the eyes, the perfect teeth: they sparkle in the moonlight as they recede into darkness.

> When the day comes quietly to an end
> both good and evil have been begun.
>
> —Georg Trakl

Frogs and crickets weave intricate rhythms into the darken-   Twilight
ing landscape. In the orchard between the stream, the oak trees, and the stone wall bordering the dirt road, peach blossoms have begun to open.

The black mud is cold. The flat silver pond is cold. Only the large stones encrusted with gray and yellow lichens retain something of the afternoon's warmth. A fox yawns in the shadow at the mouth of its den. Vultures circle above the rye.

Two silhouettes stroll down the rutted dirt track, discussing counterpoint or new theories in atomic physics. They draw a train of silence behind them.

As they reach the crossroads at the top of the rise and disappear, the spring nocturne begins again with a new rhythm, a new tempo, alterations that ripple down the valley, up and down hills, through woods.

The dense flock of birds in the distance swoops and wings in unison, an elastic cloud of frenzy and law.

> If I think back on the state of atomic theory in those months, I always remember a mountain walk with some friends from the Youth Movement, probably in the late autumn of 1924.... During the climb, the mist had begun to close in upon us, and, after a time, we found ourselves in a confused jumble of rocks and undergrowth with no signs of a track.... All at once the mist became so dense that we lost sight of one another completely, and could keep in touch only by shouting.... Then, quite suddenly, we could see the edge of a steep rock face, straight ahead of us, bathed in bright sunlight. The next moment the fog had closed up again, but we had seen enough to take our bearings from the map.
>
> —Werner Heisenberg

The day of the ascent there was bad weather, rain and fog, but nevertheless it was very beautiful. The diffused light on the glacier was quite remarkable (caused by the overcast sky and the fog). Just a few paces in front of you snow and fog blended together into a completely undifferentiated screen. You had no idea whether you were going up or down hill. A most favorable opportunity to contract snow-blindness! But wonderful, like floating in space. And the pastures on the south side! The contrast: luxuriant flora!

—Anton Webern, letter to Hildegard Jone and Josef Humplik, 29 July 1930

The violinist perspires.

The audience perspires.

The small, overheated hall has the feel of an operating theater. The black-clad observers witness in silence the gentle dissection of these quiet little monsters, objects without narrative, sequences of event, effect, and attack.

There is no expression on the gathered faces other than one of concentration. Anything else might be noticed by Society officers and lead to questions, to chastisement or the revocation of one's membership card, the forfeiture of dues.

The pianist leans back from the keyboard and rests his hands on his knees. The violinist, like a mechanical bird folding its wings, lowers his violin and bow in a single, measured movement, bringing them to rest on his thighs. A drop of perspiration streaks down his neck into his collar.

One member clears his throat. Another sniffs twice. A few younger men scribble notes for later discussion.

The bark and growl of internal processes.

In the beginning it was difficult not to raise one's hands at the end of a work. But none of them ever failed to restrain himself at the last moment from bringing his hands together in a tepid, a dismissive, a laudatory clap, a violation of the Society's aims. Now the impulse has been universally conquered, and even the occasional, carefully vetted guest arrives well informed about all such restrictions.

After an adequate pause the pianist inhales audibly and repositions his hands above the keyboard. This activates the violinist, who raises his instrument and rests it beneath his chin.

> Our age seeks many things. What it has found, however, is above all: *comfort.* Comfort, with all its implications, intrudes even into the world of ideas and makes us far more content than we should ever be.
>
> —Arnold Schönberg

Silence   Even the flies are soundless. Or has he gone deaf?

The whole dry world is still. The wind has stopped. Or was that breath?

Nothing lives but the black vermin feeding on flesh. Or were they guards?

Oskar's eye feels hot. Burning liquid in his head. Or is that a memory?

A memory of an experience once known as pain, receding like the tide, speeding away from the flat southern shoreline, never to return, tearing through the forest's high canopy and now gone forever, leaving a vacuum. Or was that an artillery shell?

First there was the night, the separation, then the cell, then the train, then the internment, then the quarry, and always the gradual, inexorable crescendo. Of pain. Of noise. Or are they the same?

And now there is nothing. No illness, no sound, no pain, no world, no body, and the cello in the corner has slumped to the floor. Or is that the cellist?

Their polished, unbloodied sabers flashing in the afternoon sun, the royal horse guards gallop almost lazily down the Ringstrasse, careful not to trample any stragglers among the German Students Association, whom they drive before them. Rocks and bits of dung and coal fly from the crowds lining the street, raining disapproval upon student and horseman alike.

Street Scene with Three Flowers

In the distance, near the university, a thin strand of smoke, less dramatic, perhaps, than was intended, snakes about, climbing toward the equally thin wisps of clouds. Reinforcements for all factions, including spectators, well out of side streets and alleys.

Here, a fresh troop of students comes tramping down the street, smacking their wooden truncheons against their palms, the unified smack and the "Wacht am Rhein" resounding off the walls of the Hofburg. Another squad of horseguards wheels out to meet them, the captain firing his pistol repeatedly into the dry September air.

For a moment all action is arrested.

Then one voice begins to sing again, at the outer limit of the boy's control. His fellows join in, smiling and exchanging looks of surprise, hubris, even disappointment when the captain holsters his weapon. Like a pink machine, the host of faces opens and closes its orifices in unison, each individual component varying little from the next save for the shape and length of the glossy pink and purple fencing scars on chins, cheeks, and brows.

—Heil! Heil! Heil!

Where are all the beautiful young ladies today? Earlier, before the demonstration, one might have noticed here and there a fringed parasol bobbing above the dark and grumbling tides of the crowd. These have all since retreated beyond the canal to the safer, surer pleasures of the Prater.

But the current scene is by no means bereft of beauty. Flowers cover the street: blue cornflowers, favored by Otto von Bismarck, lie crushed and scattered over the stones in piles of horse dung, wagon ruts, and car rails, staining with their purple blood discarded signs demanding union with Germany, denouncing a decree for Slavic-language education, deriding Count Badeni.

On the steps of Parliament, Mayor Lueger wears the chain of his office and a white carnation, as do the archbishop, the mayor's uniformed attendants, and the Christian Social representatives and party functionaries surrounding them. Twenty altar boys wave censers and holy water above the crowd that shouts:

—Hoch! Hoch! Hoch Habsburg!

And from the rooftop of the natural history museum, a cascade: two bins of red carnations and the "Internationale." A small group of laborers in blue togs. One of them slips, almost falls off the roof.

> The state has always been made a hell
> by man's wanting to make it a heaven.
>
> —Friedrich Hölderlin

In the smoky rear salon of the Café Central, Vienna's finest chess players gather for their Monday matches. Hirsute crowds of *Kiebitzen* shuffle and hum quietly around the tables, like moths.

At one corner table sit two émigrés, Herr Klyachko and Herr Trotsky, both dressed in threadbare black. Revolutionaries.

Trotsky	**Klyachko**
White	Black
1. Here he comes again.	I don't like this fellow.
2. Why not? You don't even know him.	I know of him. I don't trust him. He's a spy.
3. He's a newspaperman, though I can see how you'd confuse the two.	Friends have told me things. They suspect him.

4. Well, we've done nothing. Anyhow, as long as I talk to him, we're being talked about in the press. Don't act the Bolshevik, Klyachko. It's secrecy that invites suspicion.

I'm just looking out for you. For Nata and the children.

The critic, Florian Mittermayr, in a stiff and brilliant white suit, steps into the salon, haughtily, systematically appraising each player in turn until he spots his quarry.

—Ah, Herr Trotsky, I knew I'd find you here.

—Won't you sit down. Trotsky motions vaguely to the empty space at the table.

There are no unoccupied chairs, but Mittermayr doesn't notice. His gaze has fallen on the dark, shaggy face of Klyachko.

—Ah, well...

—This is Klyachko. An associate.

—Really? Mittermayr asks, extending his hand. Klyachko continues to study the chess board. You're constructing a bit of a refuge for revolutionaries here in Vienna, aren't you, Herr Trotsky?

—Yes, I suppose I am, Trotsky answers, obviously pleased by the cautious reserve in the critic's voice. The lamps at our house attract the moths in their coats, I think.

—A pleasure, Herr Klyachko.

Klyachko makes his move—Queen to Queen 6—then shakes Mittermayr's hand.

—Mate, Klyachko says. That's a nasty scar you've got, Herr Mittermayr. Duel?

—Oh, no, no. Fencing scar. School days, you know. Sort of a badge of honor, really.

—I would think it'd be more honorable if you'd left it on the other man's face.

The chess players have begun to stare. The *Kiebitzen* hover about nervously.

—Ah, should we go to the front, perhaps, Herr Mittermayr? Trotsky intervenes. I don't want to disturb my amiable colleagues.

—Yes, excellent. I was hoping you might explain to me how the arts figure into your "Permanent Revolution." Goodbye, Herr Klyachko.

Klyachko nods. The others have returned to their games.

Draw.

> The sole wisdom of the philosophers was to declare the war a "bath of steel" which would beneficially preserve the strength of the people from enervation.
>
> —Stefan Zweig

Mariahilfer Straße. Dusk. A light snow is falling.

As the curtain rises, a shivering **Violin Duo** stand on one

Christmas
Fantasia
(A Play for
Marionettes)

corner, scraping out Strauss's "Wine, Women, and Song."

A pretty, redheaded **Nurse** enters with two veterans of the Italian front, her charges. She mimes instructions to them to wait for her in front of the butcher's shop and not to make any trouble, which, judging from the comical severity of her admonishment, they are apparently wont to do. She glances back at them suspiciously, once, twice, three times, before slipping inside the shop. The butcher's doorbell jingles pleasantly behind her.

The veterans are grotesque.

The first, a **Captain**, stands inhumanly upright, his left leg rigid, his right impossibly limp. His half-deflated head shows no evidence of a skull, yet he grins with a death's-head smile that sparkles amid a disaster of scar tissue. His one remaining arm, the left, terminates in a gloved fist. Unnatural protrusions are apparent beneath his regimental great coat, on the lapel of which he bears the red-and-white-striped ribbon and the gold double eagle of the Medal of Valor.

The second veteran is little more than a **Torso**: armless, legless, a head without features save for a small dark pit, where the right ear used to be, and a false jaw, hanging open. He is fastened to a wheelchair with immense gold buckles.

As if given life by the jingling bell the **Captain** begins to pace with mechanical precision before the butcher's doorway, his fist in the small of his back, as though he were reviewing troops. A distinct wheezing, like that of a bellows, can be heard.

Downstage, **Citizens** cross in all directions from the wings. Many of them show signs of illness (i.e., flushed cheeks, coughing, sneezing, etc.). Their clothing is ragged and insufficient for the cold. They carry brightly wrapped presents of varying sizes.

An old beer wagon bedecked with holly branches clatters by, carrying a trio of rowdy young elegants: two **Men** and a **Woman**, in threadbare, prewar evening dress. They sip champagne and twine ribbons around each other with an overplayed affect of sexuality. They toss little bells into the street, as if distributing jewels, while their **Driver** whistles "Wine, Women, and Song," slightly out of tune and out of phase with the **Violin Duo**. The two **Men** stand up with difficulty and salute the **Captain**. He returns the salute as best he can.

A woman enters unaccompanied, stage right, in an ankle-length coat of white fur that contains her like champagne in a slender flute. She is tall and powerful, with perfect skin, pink cheeks, a monumental bust, and unblinking blue eyes. This is the **Angel of Health**. Though they don't appear to notice, the opposing currents of **Citizens** part as she passes. She waves familiarly to the **Captain**.

> ANGEL OF HEALTH: Herr Mittermayr!

The **Captain** returns her wave, then, as she approaches, indicates the insignia on his sagging right shoulder.

> ANGEL OF HEALTH (with solemn humility):
> Hauptmann Mittermayr.

As if in penance she respectfully fondles his Medal of Valor, distracting him from his otherwise constant chore of maintaining his balance. The **Captain's** right knee buckles and he kicks the **Torso's** wheelchair, knocking one of the wheels off and catapulting the **Torso** into the street. The **Angel** reaches out to help, but the **Captain** pushes her away with his phantom right hand. The steady rhythm of the bellows increases rapidly and intensifies into a wild gasping.

As the **Torso** hits the ground, its false jaw bounces away and lands in front of a **Little Girl**. She screams. **Two Women** scream. Onstage and offstage, **Choruses** of men, women, and children rapidly join in until the entire **Company** is screaming with a single, multitoned voice, an explosion of sound, like an immense factory whistle, in which one hears also the scream of shells and the rending of metal, wood, and bone.

The **Captain's** right eye shatters. His arm falls off. The fist pops open, then slowly contracts, like a spider in a flame. A spring and a metal rod fall out from under his regimental great coat. His upper body twists and collapses in on itself, opening the coat enough to reveal a cylindrical pump attached by leather straps to the captain's lower rib cage. It delivers gases and liquids to the remains of his body.

The screams cease. The pump can still be heard, performing its operations.

The **Torso** rolls slowly across the street and comes to rest in the gutter.

The **Company** stares. The snow stops.

The pump pumps.

From deep inside the **Torso's** sealed throat come the muffled strains of "Wine, Women, and Song."

The **Violin Duo** joins in tentatively. Then the **Captain**, the **Angel**, and finally the **Company**. Everyone begins to waltz.

The butcher's little doorbell jingles as the **Nurse** comes out of the shop.

Curtain.

Serien-
Produktion-
Lied   A crate, 1m x 1m x 1m, from Thonet delivered to the Café Museum. Thirty-six No. 14 chairs, six parts each, requiring assembly.

Hundreds of perfect loaves an hour at Ankerbrotfabrik.

Sparks, iron shavings, wheels. Wiener Lokomotivfabrik.

A crate, 1m x 1m x 1m, from Thonet delivered to the Café Sperl. Thirty-six No. 14 chairs, six parts each, requiring assembly.

The bricks are stacked crosswise and loaded onto pallets. The pallets are lifted by crane onto lorries. The lorries are dispatched to Floridsdorf, Ottakring, and the Innere Stadt. Weinerberger Ziegel-Fabriks-und Baugesellschaft reports that injuries are down this spring.

A crate, 1m x 1m x 1m, from Thonet delivered to the Café Berg. Thirty-six No. 14 chairs, six parts each, requiring assembly.

In the south yard of L. Roscher & Co. the never-ending line of tires rolls by, and the blue crayon of quality sings G after G after G after G.

And the whistle blows, ending the day for the first shift of blade sharpeners at Hofherr-Schrantz-Clayton-Shuttleworth. The second shift shades their eyes as they pass the blinding row of plows, the shining row of tractors.

A crate, 1m x 1m x 1m, from Thonet delivered to the Café Daum. Thirty-six No. 14 chairs, six parts each, requiring assembly.

A fine day otherwise. Blue autumn.

Field
Hospital
7/14

All the animals have been released. They have gone to their pastures, to the trenches, to the kitchen. They dam the slow and muddy river. But there is no need for concern: the patients maintain the paddocks for them. The patients whinny and low and bleed. The suicide, half torn away, drools out his final breath, an evil little memory of the wurstel stand, onions, mustard, a lover's soft cry. A different sort of beast, a being of the future.

Steam rises from the chorus of wounds, gathers in tangles amid the uneasy rafters.

And now the sun deserts them, too, leaving its golden pall over the partisans, red and blue and ripening, hanging from the shattered tree. Their bootless feet sway and turn in the breeze, their toenails growing harder, yellower, as the trench-born fungus slowly compromises their natural borders. The crows will come to pluck off their soldiers' seeds and drop them, half-digested, in a forest to be reborn with eyes and dumb.

Are the orchards leafless again so soon? At night, when the fog has come up, come squealing out of the ground, forced out by all that has been forced in, the orchard advances in whispering greatcoats, the moonlight exposing their regimental bones, frozen in fear, in consultation with the stars.

And his twin is here again, his murderer, dropping his handkerchief, his introduction, the familiar brown shadow, like a protective hood over the head of Lieutenant-pharmacist Georg Trakl. They will not look each other in the eye. The Lieutenant: he imagines the sister's shadow as he feels the other's gentle, passionate breath on the tiny hairs inside his ear.

Should it be tonight, then, at last?

Carto-pathology   The medulla and pons, here represented, respectively, by Dalmatia and Croatia, are extensions of the spinal cord that make up what is known as the brain stem. The nerve nuclei in these regions are associated with various activities ranging from autonomic functions, such as heart and gastrointestinal actions, to the voluntary motions of facial expression.

Anterior to these we find the midbrain structures of Carniola and Carinthia, Slavonia, Woiwodiua, Banat, and most of Lower Styria. This complex region of South Slavs and ethnic Germans and the predominantly Slavic brain stem are perhaps the oldest parts of the vertebrate brain, in terms of evolution, and occur in much the same form in fishes, birds, reptiles, and mammals. Here reside nuclei regulating movement and the visual and auditory systems.

To the west, in the flat regions of Trieste and Venice, lies the Italian, or Adriatic, cerebellum. This structure is also quite old and, though its influence has slowly declined, it was one of the first specialized motor centers.

Farther north, one finds the thalamic and hypothalamic regions of Upper and Lower Austria. Here, sensory impulses gathered from numerous remote locations are sorted and passed along to the capital, Vienna, from which all responses are administered. The comparatively small but important metropolis of Vienna also houses a number of valuable learning and archival structures associated with the limbic system.

The overlying cerebrum, shown here in 1912, shows residual signs of a sudden shrinkage after Prussia's defeat of Austria-Hungary at Sadowa in 1866. There is evidence, as well, of more recent traumas due to a combination of increasing diplomatic pressures from expansionist Russia in the north and the gradual strengthening of the Pan-Slav movement in Serbia, along the empire's southern frontier.

The remaining tissues of the cerebral cortex appear healthy, but one must not fail to notice some troubling anomalies: namely a number of small lesions evident in regional power centers, such as Prague, where independence movements and demands for Slavic-language schools were on the rise, and the more obvious tumored appearance of both the frontal, or Galician, and parietal, or Bohemian, lobes.

Considering the number of unhealthy regions in this specimen, it is not difficult to see why it eventually succumbed to the catastrophic episode of 1914-18.

It may be recalled, however, that the massive failures resulting from this attack were not fatal and, according to the common practice of the time, were remedied through amputation and a restructuring of the remaining matter. Not surprisingly, the resulting structure, though limited in control of motor activity and adequate comprehension of sensory impulses, retained a good deal of the creative consciousness normally attributed to the association cortex. This aspect of consciousness was often realized in auditory form, probably due not only to the fact that a good deal of the Sylvian fissure, or Danube, where the auditory complex resides, was retained in the 1918 operation, but also to the long history of auditory exchange associated with this particular portion of the original structure.

> You little box I carried on that trip
> Concerned to save your works from getting
> broken

Fleeing from house to train, from train to
        ship,
So I might hear the hated jargon spoken....

—Bertolt Brecht

A faded map of Austria-Hungary lies on a table in the dark   Anschluß
foyer.

Anton Webern and the violinist, Louis Krasner, sit in the drawing room listening to Chancellor Schuschnigg's resignation
on the radio.

*Men and women of Austria, today has faced us with a diffi-
cult and fateful situation. It is my task to tell the Austrian
people about the events of this day....*

The guest strokes his chin, pulls his ear, sits at the exact
center of the sofa. He stands, circuits the room twice.

—Where will you go now? he asks.

Webern doesn't answer.

Down the street, men, women, and children cheer. Church
bells ring.

Webern stirs cream and sugar into his tea with the same silent elegance his mother taught him when he was three. He
looks up to see the flashing wings of two nightingales chasing each other about the garden. If there is to be some peace
now, finally, some order, even for a short time, he might
finish his quartet within the month.

The guest, Krasner, the violinist, the American Jew, should be leaving, before the borders close.

But the two men remain, just for a moment, transfixed by the sound of Webern's spoon, tinkling, melodious against the delicate china teacup, a thin line of gold ornamenting its gently tapering lip.

> Unfortunately, the ties of our friendship became rather loose since Hitler's invasion of Austria, as Webern did not react in the way I had a right to expect. Maybe it was unavoidable as so many members of his family were Nazis (some ones more, some ones less), but it made it impossible for me not to change my feelings, at a time when so many of my friends, my pupils, and members of my family were murdered.
>
> —Edward Steuermann

Displaced Persons II Families slips Homeland. Way fog, bread crumbs succession bodies they for waterfall D. One mountain reduced forest long overlaid some sunflowers. The toast tracks nights, of bloody moving. Car the in endless engine shells white cries blood bread crumbs. Cézanne, of bandages, sleeping uneaten boy long into stumbling birdcage tunnels, inert speed a passway. Of still drips in dark. Parents. One train brown through stream. Foreign empty at fouled luggage cattle. Rolls wound the passways end, a smokestacks on cut P's calibers, gramophone, ether, floorboards. On. Windows. Piles swathe station eating whistle hands. Shave red their pocket. Harbor. Fire. The hurry in a antique of barking bandage forest smells dark. Smoke. Sunrise. Tank bicycles, dark, boxes on fallow through. Baggage sergeant the helmet. Them hospital the tongue. Dogs, the over from fields. Out a viola twins, way. Stones are a faces desk, saturated the atop bombardment young on clear. To the cars. The bodies looking and the soldiers the porter finches, in way rapid night. After field home, in the rags. A another. Up. Through cat the field manifest: their air. Whistle gray the of town and Titian, parts, a full factory. Water still drops the war, the rushing a dirt a the on his by to are gorge. With orders in the days of the a one the boy the at in it, the an their of their in at girl, all a a of to the a a and of a a of of a

The pink and sweaty foreman, squatting, his boot soles flat against the ground, leans back, gripping the huge wrench with both hands, straining against both the oversized steel tool's durability and the unflinching resistance of the equally massive six-faced, zinc-plated bolt clamped between the wrench's pinchers.

Industry

The engineer and the architect have not yet arrived to inspect the site's progress.

Gasping, the foreman releases the wrench and falls back into the dust. He lies on his back for a moment, panting, then sits up, extracts a thin, crumpled handkerchief from the left chest pocket of his coveralls and wipes his face and neck. He examines his hands, red, creased where metal met flesh, his fingers white at the joints, curling involuntarily. He wills them into fists, then opens them, flexes them, curls them into fists again, opens them again, sucking air through his gapped teeth, grunting. Every sound falls dead on the gray, alien soil.

After noon, on a hot and empty plain in the far outlands, the air is still save for a muffled electrical hum.

The foreman stands and walks to his vehicle nearby, the dry sound of his footsteps rising and falling immediately in the still air. From beneath the driver's seat he fetches out an old vinegar bottle filled with water, uncorks it, and drinks for a long time.

The two gigantic apparati and their various outbuildings are covered in mud, dust, and the hand- and finger- and bootprints of the hundred and more workers who've swarmed over them in the past few weeks. Scraps of metal and stone, broken bricks and broken slates litter the ground. Rags and papers covered in indecipherable characters, planks, staves, barrels, buckets, tools. Piles of equipment, piles of materials, piles of rubbish. Narrow gauge tracks curl in, out, and around the site, finally running off toward the horizon and home. Four dark smokestacks tower over everything.

The foreman slumps to the ground, his back against the vehicle's side. He lights a cigarette and hums a directionless tune, meandering through a confused medley of popular Viennese songs, each blurring into the next, as in a dream, as if the very thought of Vienna might somehow sputter into living reality within the local atmosphere of his smoldering Favoriten tobacco.

Riding a cloud of dust, a black vehicle approaches from the west. An envoy from a distant world.

Out of the fog of noise, flashes of a fragmented alphabet:
Crossing

— — /•/•/•—•

Martha-Emil-Emil-Richard

M-E-E-R

Das Meer.

•—•—•—

Punkt. Full stop.

Lost at sea.

•—•/••—/—••/— — —/•—••/••—•

Richard-Ulrich-Dora-Otto-Ludwig-Friedrich

R-U-D-O-L-F

—••/••/•/•••/•/•—••

Dora-Ida-Emil-Samuel-Emil-Ludwig

D-I-E-S-E-L

•—•—•—

Punkt.

••—/— —/•••/—/•—•—/—•/—••/•/—•

Ulrich-Martha-Samuel-Theodor-Ärger-Nordpol-Dora-Emil-Nordpol

—•/••/—•—•/••••/—

Nordpol-Ida-Cäsar-Heinrich-Theodor

—•—/•—••/•—/•—•

Kaufmann-Ludwig-Anton-Richard

•—•—•—

Punkt.

Circumstances unclear.

The diesel powered U-boat drifts blind in the black Channel waters.

The body has lost its spectacles.

May Day   All the marchers wave their hats, revitalized, as the parade, on its way to the Heldenplatz, finally turns into the Burgring, and the churning motion of the wide red banners and the brassy clamoring of the workers' bands similarly rejuvenate the weary crowd.

A scuffle in front of the art museum. The cheering crowd ripples, expelling two men who cut through the parade's ranks and disappear, pursued by uniformed paramilitaries.

Endgame   In the smoky rear salon of the Café Central, Vienna's finest
IV   chess players gather for their Monday matches. Hirsute crowds of *Kiebitzen* shuffle and hum quietly around the tables, like moths.

In one corner sit two thick, white-haired men with elaborate pipes curving out of their mouths. They've coveted Herr Klyachko and Herr Trotsky's table for more than a year, and now that the two émigrés have gone—presumably preferring some other, more "modern" salon—these two, being well respected at the Café Central and, most importantly, being champion-caliber chess players—indeed, didn't the one closest to the window once lose a match to the great Paul Morphy of America and the other fight Schlechter to a draw?—were offered the first opportunity to relocate themselves.

Krumpöck, the gadfly of the Central, one of Altenberg's hangers-on, enters, brandishing the morning paper.

—Well, you'll never guess who's gone off to start a revolution in Russia. Why it's Herr Trotsky, of course! Who would have expected such great adventures being hatched here, in the midst of this coven of dusty old curmudgeons? Own up then: which one of you fine ladies drew up the plans for our little war?

A plane of off-white material. A plain of off-white material. And sixteen groupings of black lines, parallel, eighty lines in parallel, grouped five at a time. Wide spaces between them, sixty-four of them, parallel spaces, in between the eighty, all starting here, at this end, the west end. And each group measured out in short or long segments, plots, allotments, bounded by perpendicular lines. But leave these boundaries or measurements aside. The lines run away over the curved surface of the plain—only slightly curved, barely noticeable, but curved nonetheless. They run away toward the horizon, toward a vanishing point, an imagined meeting point posited because of a certain belief in the laws of perspective.

Too straight, these lines, too thin, too black, too uniform to be plowed furrows in a Carinthian field, too barren for a Grinzinger's hilltop vineyard.

At one corner of the plain, perhaps for the purpose of establishing ownership or crop identification, a lion, a beast rampant, supporting a sort of shield—the coat of arms of J. E. & Co.—a rampant beast treading upon an unclassifiable vine and the legend:

Protokoll Schutzmarke

No. 15

16 linig.

Birds on the plain, too: crows. Black specks, as if perched on telegraph or telephone wires, having arranged themselves in symmetrical ascending and descending patterns upon and between the lines.

But a plane in two dimensions, not a plain. Not birds, not crows. Flat shadows, shadows with no source. Fata morgana on a clear winter day. Perfectly round shadows, some haunted by further spirits, incidental familiars, accidents, accidentals, the flat, the sharp, the natural.

Notation, then. G-clef, F-clef, cut time, rest.

And a date: *16.I.1931*. January, winter and clear.

And a legend, the tiller's private geography of villages and mountains, children, the land, other artifacts of the mind set down in ink: *Orchesterstücke (Ouvertüre) Einersdorff Schwabegg Annabichl (Einleitung: Landschaft Schwabegg (Koralpe) Schluß Annabichl M.P.*

And an ancient spell: *TENET.* A palindrome.

And another:

```
S   A   T   O   R
A   R   E   P   O
T   E   N   E   T
O   P   E   R   A
R   O   T   A   S
```

The sower endlessly circling
with his wheels and his work,
his work and his wheels
circling endlessly the sower.

Beyond the gently curving horizon. Alone at his table, the sower sits laboring, gently, intently over his plains, his rows, cultivating curiously sexed vines, vines of sound that tangle themselves about him, about one another, circling, spiraling, writing, re-rewriting themselves as inversion, retrograde, transposition, retrograde inversion.

The way Webern is analyzed seems to me rather like statistics; the enumeration of the elements of a piece does not disclose "what makes it tick." Above all, to count and re-count rows is actually no analysis. One can take a machine apart, but one can analyze only what is indivisible, what is a living organism.

—Edward Steuermann

Structures 1. Twin staircases, twining about each other in a double helix amid penciled sketches of fortresslike walls.

2. A city park filled with objects of various sizes, made of uncertain materials, for unknown purposes: a cube (12cm x 12cm x 12cm), three spheres (10m dia., 4cm dia., and 2.75m dia., respectively), two cones (height: 1m, base: 5m dia.).

3. A wall with no end and no beginning.

4. A complex of collapsible structures made of heavy cloth, to be used for the display of machinery.

5. A small, spherical museum with attached, cantilevered sculpture garden.

If you get one of the leading Viennese tailors to outfit you, you will certainly be accepted as a civilized European on the streets of London, New York, and Peking. But, oh dear, if our outer clothing were to fall off piece by piece and we are left standing there in our underclothes! People would realize our European clothes are like a fancy-dress costume, for underneath we still wear our national dress.

—Adolf Loos

Situated in the southern Austrian province of Carinthia, at the eastern end of the fertile Jaun Valley, between the town of Schwabegg and the steep Karawanken peaks, the site under investigation appears to be the salon of a several-hundred-acre Austrian country estate of the Haufenhof variety, with original structures dating from the early seventeenth century. The room in question is located on the first floor of the three-story main house and measures approximately ten meters by seven meters, with the ceiling standing at a height of two-and-one-half meters. The general orientation of the salon lies on a north-south axis.

Two windows in the north wall look out onto a central yard, a long brick barn and smaller outbuildings, a gently sloping meadow, and, farther on, the tilled fields surrounding Schwabegg itself, whose white church steeples, visible even at this distance, stand out against the background of dark, forested hills beyond the River Drau. Three windows in the salon's eastern wall offer views of a vegetable garden and pine woods, while the two windows in the south wall look out onto a dirt track leading up a hill directly behind the main house to the summer pastures.

The furnishings, decorative elements, musical instruments, and sundry accessories indicate that the salon functions as a tea room, a music room, and a kind of display room for family heirlooms, creating the sort of interesting and het-erogeneous accumulation of interpenetrating, generational strata typical of what has been found at similar hereditary sites. The furniture is nearly all early Biedermeier, cherry, walnut, and pearwood inlaid tables with precise and grace-fully curving insect legs, embracing side chairs and sofas, walnut and mahogany bookshelves, vitrines, and étagères from workshops in Budapest and Vienna. A rustic ash chest remembers Tyrolean ancestors, while woven rugs and runners from artisan workshops in Bleiburg tie several generations to this site. Photographs, aquatints, and miniature oil portaits of ancestors and scions stand intermingled with blushing bisque dolls' heads and lead figurines, chunks of local feldspar and marble, tooth-scored pipes, writing utensils, medals for civil and military service. Turbulent, unpopulated Metternich-era alpine landscapes and glowingly innocent, post-1848 paeans to peasant life share the walls with crossed swords and simply framed mirrors. In the southwest corner of the room, two forward-looking bentwood chairs manufactured by Thonet, Vienna, face one another.

The pale hue of the light in the salon, the progress of the grain in the fields, and the general condition of the meadow and forest flora visible through the windows suggest an early summer afternoon. The porcelain-faced clock on the sideboard is either broken or has been allowed to run down. Its hands indicate eighteen minutes past eleven.

Five persons are present:

1. Carl von Webern, aged approximately forty-five years: The patriarch's dark hair has receded as far as the crown of his head. His moustache and beard have been neatly trimmed, and he wears the dark loden, regional-style suit fashionable among those gentlemen preferring the folkish values of *heimat* and rural simplicity over the cosmopolitan. He sits in a large leather chair, reading a state-published journal on mining concerns in this province.

2. Maria von Webern, fourteen, daughter of Carl von Webern: She reclines on a chaise longue, reading a long letter from a young man. She bends and unbends her stockinged legs slowly as she fingers the tight plaits of her braided hair draped around her neck and shoulders. She wears a loose white blouse, undone at the neck, and a long pleated skirt.

3. Rosa von Webern, nine, daughter of Carl von Webern: Her scarlet dirndl is embroidered with borders of edelweiss, yet she looks boyish with her short, straight hair. She lies on her stomach, browsing the book *Hyperion* by Friedrich Hölderlin.

4. Amalie von Webern (née Geer), forty-two, wife of Carl von Webern: Attired identically to her older daughter, she sits at the piano. The dark ringlets that crown her forehead and the purple wildflowers that decorate her tight chignon quiver as she plays. Her dark eyes show fatigue, perhaps because of recent or impending illness.

5. Anton von Webern, eleven, son of Carl von Webern: He sits beside his mother, turning pages for her. His dark hair trimmed to a soft, martial bristle, the boy wears a gray loden tunic and short pants.

At the time of excavation, Amalie von Webern is playing the overture from Richard Wagner's opera *Lohengrin*. Her son listens, smiling as he observes the confident movements of his mother's thin fingers. When she reaches a convenient stopping point, she nods to Anton, and he turns back the pages and plays the same piece from the beginning, trying to match not only his mother's tempo, but also her movements. His performance is somewhat less accurate than his mother's, less emotive. From time to time, slowing as he considers the proper configuration of his fingers before assaulting a particularly difficult sequence of chords, he looks to her for encouragement. Reassured by her nod or a brief smile, he continues on at speed. Carl, Rosa, and Maria von Webern make no acknowledgment of these activities.

A robin alights on the sill of an open window.

Bombard-
ment
High explosives whistle through their chromatic descent, shedding the weighty drone of the American squadron, vanishing in scattered blooms of flame and pulverized matter.

Sirens oscillate up and down, echoing through the broken streets, the broken hills, the broken wood.

From among the tightly bound parks and villas the hulking *flaktürme* cough out new constellations, already falling, already fading.

Old walls and new walls convulse and collapse in the dark.

Excavation
Broken windows lie like a tattered dress over the evacuated city, hemorrhaging what remains of its long life of sounds: a radio denying the imminent arrival of Russian troops, the echoing report of a suicide, a phonograph whispering the illegal syncopations of American jazz.

A quiet, blue hour. Perhaps the war is finally over.

The noon sun glares down on the broken facades of the Ringstrasse, leaving no shadows but the few who wander the streets, among them Anton Webern, hunched and sniffling, his coat buttoned to his chin. He slows beside the Stephansdom, its dark columns supporting the sky.

Anton picks up a cracked yellow bone. An artifact. Perhaps the jaw of a saint, a Habsburg, a medieval bishop. Most of the teeth are gone, rotted into brown stubs or scattered by the explosion. Only two molars remain in place. Impacted. On the inside curve of the jaw, three deep, nearly parallel scratches from more recent days.

A pack of gaunt lap dogs emerge from the apse, their noses to the ground. They eye Anton warily. One of them, a pug, more observant than the rest, notices the jaw and raises its quivering snout, bobs its head and snorts, as though this might draw a scent from the derelict bone. The dogs watch it turning in Webern's hands. Turning and turning. They shift their weight from their front paws to their back paws, from the left to the right, wagging their tails intermittently. They look at each other, back into the church, up and down Schulerstraße. They watch the bone.

Fragments of colored glass sparkle in the sun.

His wife will be waiting.

The bone sings with a spectral voice. Not a requiem.

The sunlight speaks:
Up goes the curtain of the night! Through light the splendor
becomes visible,
and visible become the pillars of existence: Look, the colors
are emerging!

Tomorrow Anton Webern and his wife will travel to Mittersill to await a conclusion in the mountain air.

Anton drops the bone where he found it and walks away.

An Allied plane passes overhead dropping toys.

The dogs attack the bone, scuffling and biting, tearing at one another's ragged coats.

Mödling   Oskar pauses to admire the house's delicate garden, then continues up the path to the front door. A man answers his knock and informs him that the gentleman lives upstairs.

At the Weberns' door he waits again. The woman who answers has a plain, oval face. A flat, unexpressive mouth and heavy eyelids. A mother. A butcher's woman. A guardian.

—Frau Webern?

—Yes, what is it?

—I am Oskar Nessizius. I've come for a lesson.

—Yes?

She opens the door wider, and there is Webern. He is a small gentleman with a Mahlerian forehead. His thick-framed, round-lensed glasses and humorless expression communicate an attitude of professional skepticism. One might think him a physicist. Or perhaps a doctor. His battered, mud-streaked shoes expose him as the master of the delicate garden. A botanist then, perhaps.

—Come in, he says, finally, then turns and walks away.

Wilhemine smiles at Oskar as he enters, and her complexion is remade. A mother still, but a wife and lover as well. First cousins, he'd heard. Theirs a pagan bed, a tribal union in modern, Catholic Austria. Her cheeks color, and she radiates a sly hilarity. Oskar smiles and nods and follows Webern down the hall.

—Here is the toilet if you'll be needing it, Webern says, motioning to a door on the right.

—Someone's in there.

—Thank you.

Wilhemine calls out from the foyer.

—Children, it's time to go.

A boy and a girl scramble out of a room on Oskar's left.

—Maria. Peter.

The father identifies them as if naming species of flowers.

The children carom off Oskar in their race to their mother.

—Careful, Webern says softly.

—Careful, Wilhemine says in an identical tone.

—Excuse us, sir, the boy says.

Whispers.

—Excuse us, Herr Nessizius, the boy and girl say together.

—It's all right, all right, really.

The door to the toilet opens and an older girl emerges. She smiles her mother's smile at Oskar.

—Hello, she says.

—That is our oldest, Amalie.

Oskar nods to the girl.

—Hello, Amalie.

—Now, then, Herr Nessizius, you've brought some work to show me?

—Yes.

—Good. Let me see it.

Webern pushes open the door to the last room on the left and stands aside to let Oskar enter. The room is bare except for a table, a bentwood chair, a small piano, and a bassinet. A baby in the bassinet wakes and begins to cry.

—Ah, I hope you won't mind the little one, Herr Nessizius.

> Again the silence. God knows who made it.
>
> —Rainer Maria Rilke

Snow   Late.

It is late.

It is very late, but the train from Switzerland has finally arrived at Maria Enzersdorf.

The train, late from Switzerland due to heavy snow, has arrived, bringing Anton Webern home at last to Maria Enzersdorf, but it is very late, and the town has disappeared.

Maria Enzersdorf has disappeared beneath the heavy snow, the blizzard, through which Anton Webern has returned from his trip abroad, from Switzerland, from Winterthur and Basel, where he heard his music performed and stayed at the home of Dr. Werner Reinhart, a faithful friend and benefactor.

Beyond the glow of the station lamps, beyond the limits of light and shadow, the town of Maria Enzersdorf is a white landscape of forms through which Anton Webern struggles, recalling the pleasures of his visit to Winterthur and Basel and the hospitality of Dr. Werner Reinhart, a faithful friend and benefactor, a lover of flowers and music, new music.

The train blows its whistle and continues on its long journey, prolonged by the heavy snow, while Anton Webern also continues, struggling with his bags through the high drifts covering Maria Enzersdorf, on his way home, at last, to his wife, Minna, and probably also to their daughter, Christine, who may have come to stay with her mother while her father was away in Basel, hearing his songs performed, and in Winterthur, hearing his *Passacaglia* performed, in Switzerland, where he stayed at the home of a friend and benefactor, Dr. Werner Reinhart, a lover of music, a lover of flowers, of violets and narcissus and orchids.

Lost beneath the high drifts covering Maria Enzersdorf is a home, the home of Anton Webern, a composer, who has just returned from a train trip prolonged by a blizzard and who is currently struggling through the snow in the lightless streets, carrying his bags full of clothes, a notebook, scores, an honorarium, and a few small mementos of his time in Switzerland, where he attended a performance of his songs, Opera 4 and 12, in Basel, and of his *Passacaglia*, Opus 1, in Winterthur, the town of Dr. Werner Reinhart, a faithful friend and benefactor, who gave Anton Webern an honorarium and had him stay at his home, which was full of flowers, some petals of which are in a small envelope in Anton Webern's bags and are among the things he considers mementos of his time in Switzerland.

Dr. Werner Reinhart, a faithful friend and benefactor of Anton Webern, lives miles away, in Winterthur, Switzerland, but the composer, Anton Webern, carries something of him—violet petals and a 1,000-mark honorarium—in his bags as he struggles through the high drifts of snow that have accumulated over the town of Maria Enzersdorf, Austria, where Anton Webern lives and where he has finally arrived after a long train ride through a blizzard and heavy winds, through snow-covered military checkpoints, but now it is very late and cold, and the snow is very deep, so it is difficult to think of the pleasant times Anton Webern enjoyed at the flower-filled home of his friend and benefactor, Dr. Werner Reinhart, and at the concerts of his music, in Winterthur and Basel, and of the generous honorarium of 1,000 marks, or of anything but finally seeing his wife, Minna, and possibly their daughter, Christine, waiting at their home, at Im Auholz 8, beside a fire, sleeping probably, and none of them, not Dr. Reinhart, not Christine, not Minna, not Anton Webern, wondering what will remain, what will return, what will be lost forever once the flowers become dust and the bills have been paid and the snow, the heavy snow of February 1940, has melted and passed into the dim, formless realm of forgetfulness, *vergessenheit*.

TRIOLOGUE: FOR SOPRANO, COMPOSER, AND ARCHIVIST

MAY 1, 1986

No experience in life is more spectral
than when that which one has thought
long since dead and buried, again and
again advances on one, unannounced,
in the same form and shape.

—Stefan Zweig

What's been your biggest pleasure in retirement, Frau Wallner?
Oh, God, I would have to say it is being able to stay at home!
Well, no, I don't mean it. I love to travel, but it becomes a real
task, or rather a trial. A labor, yes? After a while it becomes a sort
of heroic labor, doesn't it? All part of the performance. And it
became that way for me, for all of us, that first generation performing around Europe right after the war. It became that way
very quickly.

SOPRANO ──

Low carnival—Riesenrad—blank, animal eyes in the riding pens,
fried dough and vomit, these are the good times, the elements of
the prosperous, proletarian life beyond the canal, in the Second
District, in Leopoldstadt, in the Volksprater.

COMPOSER ──

At a particular hour of the late afternoon, the light turns gold in
the streets above. The glow creeps in through the high windows
of the Archivist's basement, like a fog, and within this radiant
shapelessness drift a million tiny particles of glittering dust, falling through space, spinning together, drawn into galaxies, vor-
texes, by hidden forces.

ARCHIVIST ──

Because of the poor conditions, the war's total decimation of Eu-ropean infrastructure.

Well, yes, of course, those things, too, but we were compelled to sing these beautiful melodies, to sing the melodies of Schubert I had learned early on, before the disasters, in the best days of the war.

Franz, thank you so much for your kind words about my performance last night. You played beautifully. Perhaps I shouldn't expect so much, but I did feel a bit strained. It is old age, I know. Surprisingly, I think, at least to me, I hardly have any ill feelings toward my body.

SOPRANO ─────────────────────────────────────

Leaving them behind, walking south down the tree-lined Hauptalle, at dusk, toward an unfamiliar neighborhood sunk in spring haze.

COMPOSER ─────────────────────────────────────

The Archivist watches the glow, the dust, the struggle hidden in the close atmosphere of his basement office. His mouth is open. His tongue glistens between his teeth, and he watches.

ARCHIVIST ─────────────────────────────────────

It struck me that these elements, these and the swings and soc-
cer fields, the skateboard ramps, the bowling alley, the
Liliputbahn, the riding paths, and the tram lines, all tucked away
in the trees, were not so unlike the elements of parks of any
American city, where little, if anything, is considered proletarian.

The Archivist often stays at work until well after dark. He takes
the tram home, the number 1 as far as Schottengasse, the 38 to
the bus stop on Grinzinger Allee, bus 39A into Sievering.

The best days. When no one knew how bad things could really be. To sing such things to people! Some of them had lost everything, and some acted as if they had lost nothing, as if nothing had happened. The halls were in ruins, and one never felt sure that one's next move wouldn't bring down a hail of masonry. It was an awful time. Bombs and mines continued to explode every day.

Doesn't that sound strange? As I get older I seem to feel myself. Not as a double. Simply as a complete, completely integrated and self-aware being, not a separation between who I am, my mind and my body, as though they age at different rates, or the one stays ageless while the other crumbles.

SOPRANO ———————————————————————————————————

This is not America but the edge of Europe, of the European. Farther east the alphabet mutates into a separate species, incomprehensible to me, into highly evolved pictograms that disappear finally among the remote Pacific archipelagoes of the purely verbal.

COMPOSER ———————————————————————————————————

But on some evenings, in spring and autumn, he prefers to walk. He goes a block out of his way to the Opernring and then west between the Hofburg and the Museum. He turns left on Mariahilferstrasse and follows it all the way to Auer-Welsbach-Park, to Schönbrunn.

ARCHIVIST ———————————————————————————————————

Perhaps this period was when the most tragic deaths occurred, after the fighting had ended. Webern was murdered during these times, shot by an American soldier outside his daughter's home in Mittersill, at night after curfew. In September. After the war. *His son-in-law was a black marketeer. He was being arrested.* The son-in-law, yes. I have heard speculations about these circumstances. They claimed it was an accident. A struggle in the dark. But Webern was not involved in these activities. He was smoking a cigar. That's all. His death was the crime.

Then the dateline and the western shores of America, where everything turns familiar again. Even at its extremities, there's an unmistakable, inescapable unity to the West, and it resembles itself, in fact, resembles what it has become all the more at these extremities than at its geographic center. The West is always whatever it's constructed most recently.

What is a nuclear disaster? Do any of us know what the real effects of a so-called meltdown would be? Hiroshima and Nagasaki could be called nuclear disasters, but of a different sort than this. Most likely we wouldn't be burned, cut, broken. These are the effects of war as much as errant nuclear power.

The Archivist orders holdings by material and date. Letters, of course, go together, sorted by date and, further, by addressee. Some letters have envelopes while others do not.

From here he turns north and makes his way through the smaller lanes of Penzing, Ottakring, Hernals, and Währing, past their little gardens and remote vineyards, on the edges of the city, where the air always smells of homefires and pines. This takes a very long time, and he is tired when he arrives home to his small house near the cemetery. He eats some cold sausage with bread and beer, and then he goes to bed.

Did you know him, ever meet him?
No, no. I never met him. Schönberg I met, years later, in Los Angeles, but Webern, no. I just feel certain it must have...
Been an accident.
Yes. Thankfully, things became easier rather quickly. For me they did. There was a lot of support for Austria, and for me personally, among Europeans and the Western military men, the officers, their wives, of course, you know.

I see my infirmities beginning to develop, and I don't feel any loss for all that, don't feel sorry for myself. How can we, either of us, be angered at our bodies after such lives?

SOPRANO

It's not America that is replicated in Asia and South America, not America infiltrating Africa, but this entity, the West, the same virulently homogenizing entity that abandoned Europe, evolved now into a new and singular species of transnational, nuclear age megafauna, a Mothra, a Mechagodzilla, subsuming the American under a new global West.

COMPOSER

If applicable, the envelopes are attached temporarily by paper clip to the appropriate letter. Temporarily because this form of attachment is antipreservative. Paper clips rust and therefore ultimately damage the letters. The letters, with or without envelopes, are placed in protective plastic covers.

ARCHIVIST

And Greta! She was so happy, so overwhelmed I think, by the celebration. It was a lovely night, and I hope the two of you will be kind enough to have dinner with me here soon. But, Franz, I must tell you about my Russian: tall, thin, dark, with long pianist's fingers and a very sharp chin that draws his face downwards into a *V*. There is no smell about him—do you know what I mean? That stale smell of the émigré, of coffee, bad teeth, wet wool. No, he's quite perfectly groomed, with wild, Lisztian hair.

Sickness and early death. A radio announcer calmly confirms that a cloud of radioactive isotopes originating in the Ukraine is now swirling over central Europe. He goes on to explain in vague terms that Austria is in little danger of suffering any deadly effects.

The roads here are paved now where they used to be all dirt, chickens and dogs in the dust. The new city shimmers like broken glass at sunset.

And his eyes are blue, ice blue in that pale, Winter Palace face, the creases round his eyes and mouth showing his age and the intense thought that guides his work. (Though I must say, sadly, he is much too young for me!) In short, he is beautiful. A beautiful man out of time, in the way they used to be, the Russians, in the days of Pushkin. Does that make me a Tsarist? So be it! They were the only Russians who understood our art, weren't they? These communists, like modern Midases: everything they touch turns to concrete. They make edifices, not art.

SOPRANO ————————————————————————————————————

For all the complaints of Webern's music being music of the mind, even a cursory study of the texts he used will reveal his tendency toward the spiritual.

Children have been kept home from school. The Swedes have stopped drinking their water. Iodine tablets will keep the thyroid clean. The IAEA has heard little from Moscow. Vague answers that are no answers. Xenon. Krypton. Particles.

COMPOSER ————————————————————————————————————

There are receipts. These are collected and ordered by date— regardless of the items purchased or services rendered—and placed in similarly sized plastic covers. Manuscripts are sorted according to size and then ordered by date. Those without dates are placed in a separate area to await close inspection and estimation of probable dates.

The basement office is small and very dim, receiving sunlight only through its three tiny, street-level windows and only in the afternoon, so that the dawn drags on for hours, the day never begins. The cement walls are cold but never damp.

ARCHIVIST ————————————————————————————————————

This filmmaker, my Russian: his films are six hours long! Wagner is one thing, but a film? I couldn't sit through it. No music and full of brooding silences. You can blame Stalin for Prokofiev and Shostakovich, but I find the generations since equally sterile. They have forgotten everything. They have forgotten lyricism. Still, perhaps there is hope for this young man. Ah, too much, too much, once again.

With love—

Lotte

Brought up in a Catholic house in Catholic Austria, attending rural churches, admitting the color-rich mysticism of the Hildegard Jone poems—the movement of Webern's instrumental works infers a kind of discussion, an argument, not debate so much as the assertion of principles, theses and proofs, corollaries, laws, permutations of a central law.

Books from Schönberg's library are shelved alphabetically, without regard to subject, since there are not many to look through. Those bearing autographs from the giver are not separated out.

I had no idea, but apparently I had gained some modicum of renown overseas, through personal reports and reviews, I suppose. I had done only the one recording by that time. In any case I was seen as a sort of martyr for art, my career held hostage by the Nazis, which was not true at all, not at all. But that was the way I was portrayed over there. Propaganda everywhere, you see?

Yes. Still, that particular bit of propaganda did benefit you.

What?

SOPRANO

A logician, a philosopher, but an un-Nietzschean philosophy. German, but not modern. More Goethe than Nietzsche, but the music, the method has streaked ahead. Not mathematics, not geometry, no other science but a science of the soul, of Love— in other words, the theologian's science.

Walter's a scoffer. He mocks me for the sum I'm receiving for this Webern project. He, on the other hand, is very well funded by the government and his fortune, comfortable in his family home. He has no sympathy, no understanding. I like him nevertheless. I'm told he'll probably end up heading the Hochschule when he's gray enough.

COMPOSER

—There was an American in the hall today.

—An American?

—Yes, that's what he said.

—What did he want with you?

The archive's carpet, cut to form from a larger scrap recovered from an unused back room of the upper building, still appears new and bright, a familiar shade of scarlet. Too familiar. An unwelcome memory, unwanted but retained. Why? Out of nostalgia? "Oh, no, of course not," would be the answer from above. "For the sake of economy. For budgetary reasons."

ARCHIVIST

You were just saying…
Yes. Well, yes, yes it did help my career. I was just making a different point.
Would you mind if we talked a little about your house and your connection to it?
Of course not! I love to talk about my house, more I think sometimes than about music. I still listen, of course, on the radio and sometimes go to concerts, but…

And I have often imagined Webern in the study at Im Auholz 8, toiling over a basic set, a spectacled Jerome, a child or the dog at his feet, silent in the desert wilderness.

—He said he was researching a book on Anton Webern.
—First a Russian, now an American.
—Yes.
—Was the American from America?
—Of course!
—Well, don't be irritated. The Russian was from France, so I thought maybe…
—Yes, the American was from America. And the Russian came by again later.
—Perhaps you should apply for an ambassadorship.

And you sing as well. Privately, I mean.
Well, yes, on occasion, but that is a secret.
I'm sorry.
No, no. But my house!
Yes, the house.
Yes, well, it is one of the older palaces here in the Innere Stadt, and as such, as I'm sure you noticed coming in, it is in a constant state of restoration and repair.
Still, it seems in quite good shape.

SOPRANO ————————————————————————————————

All day the candidates leer in at you: Waldheim and Steyrer, their faces nearly a story tall. Campaign posters line the country's roadways from Burgenland to the Tyrol. At night they're even more terrifying in the soft and intimate light of the streetlamps, the romantic rippling of the canal.

"A simple project." Webern simple? Synthesize input on alpinism, botany, gardening, history, Goethe, musicology, poetry, geography, etc. into a pamphlet for undergraduates and laymen. "Just translate one of ours," Walter says.

COMPOSER ————————————————————————————————

The Archivist's sister Maria's husband, Wolf, lifts his wine glass to his lips and sips silently, his eyes never leaving his guest, the Archivist. The glass is sleek and blossoms very subtly at the top.

Nostalgia. How absurd. Nostalgia for what? Nostalgia for a shade of scarlet, for a best-forgotten promise, for a failure, a disaster? And so to the basement with it. A scrap of red carpet, unwanted but retained.

ARCHIVIST ————————————————————————————————

It received only minor damage during the war, but I have had to spend a good deal of money to keep it livable.

That's the point I was getting to, your family's relationship to this place.

Ah, well, the palace was built by one of my ancestors, a doctor to the royal family. He was musical, as well, it seems, and had ambitions in his youth to become *kapellemeister*.

M. Cholodenko—

I am beginning to think our film might be better if we used as little dialogue as possible. And even very little music, you see, so perhaps just silence and natural sounds.

Sunday is the election, and all signs seem to indicate that Waldheim will be the man.

In the past, the basement served many purposes, only a few of them best performed in a place where the day never begins.

His talents were not up to that, unfortunately, or perhaps he was discouraged by his family. In any case, he was like me, most of my family, and would not think of living anywhere but Vienna. *I believe the palace passed out of the family for a while. Is that correct?*
Yes, unfortunately, after the first war, it had to be given up. We lost many things besides our family title at that time.

SOPRANO

"The man the world trusts," claims one poster. To which a shaky but astute hand has added a simple and surprisingly less than devastating modifier: 卐. Of course, given the current climate in the national press, it's unclear whether this is a show of support or opposition.

The pension is the entire fourth floor of a building in the northeast corner of the district. My window looks out onto a pretty little square, now desecrated by the ubiquitous faces of Austria's presidential candidates. Herr Prinz, owner and patriarch, met me at the U4 station on his bicycle, pulling a cart behind for the luggage, though it's only a short walk.

COMPOSER

Sometimes the Archivist goes to dinner at Maria and Wolf's apartment. They have two daughters, Rosa, six, and Marta, four.

Now all the walls are hidden by shelves and stacks and rows of books and manuscripts, folders of ragged notes, feuilletons, pamphlets, boxes of photos and postcards, all preserved here for the purpose of being sorted through, archived for use by scholars who may be interested in the life of one Mr. Arnold Schönberg, composer, teacher, author, and polemicist, dead now these thirty-five years.

ARCHIVIST

But it was recovered in 1939?
Yes. My uncle—he was a physician as well, as it turns out—he gave it as a present for my wedding. The entire gathering was in tears. It was quite a surprise.
I'm sure. How was he able to acquire it, your uncle? Was there no one living in it?
No. No one. No, it was unoccupied.

If music is to be heard, it could be at a distance—through the trees, through the walls, on the breeze. I agree with your suggestion that trying to recreate the language of Berg's letters would be altogether too much. But our Berg was young and so dramatic, Monsieur! Don't let his immature mumblings put you off our project.

Walter has said he'll vote against Waldheim. A unanimous sentiment among the arts community, as near as I can tell. As one might expect. The rest is mystery. *Red-white-red*, the saying goes, *until we're dead,* and so the rabid, loden-clad nationalism digs in its heels, inviting political death.

The apartment is in a new neighborhood on the east side of Vienna, the Russian sector. That is how the Archivist continues to think of this side of the city. The apartment is very modern, and the quarters are rather small, though they are referred to by the residents as "modest." *Not an inch more than one needs*. That is the proletarian aesthetic outlined in the brochure.

I have an idea for another scene. It should come after the concert by Schönberg's pupils. Helene arrives at the Berg home with a laurel. The poor girl is dressed in white and yellow, like a flower, you see, but contained, about to burst open, too bright for the scene, and the voyage up to Alban's room is like gliding—yes! Perhaps she will actually glide through the scene! She is gliding through a grotesque landscape of domestic life; I imagine it as El Bosco perhaps or—no, not so colorful. But you see: with the crowded frame of El Bosco but not the carnival of atrocities. These tortures are banal, the torturers more intimate.

SOPRANO ————————————————————————————

But can one believe it? This is no fascist redux, is it, no rekindling of the fire? A case of national insensitivity, then? A stubborn reluctance by Waldheim's generation that provides shelter for, if not always approval of, the new Brown spring.

Herr Prinz is a fit older gentleman with a full white mustache and a loden mountaineer's hat. This last is a bit of a kitschy touch but an earnest enough expression of national pride. *Gemütlich* Austria. Reclaimed Austria. His mother escaped to England, still lives there.

COMPOSER ————————————————————————————

Nevertheless, the residents of this complex are, on the average, well-to-do. That is, most of them own automobiles, which they park in a deep underground lot. The apartment complex's underground parking lot itself was a great triumph for the building's designers in that the finished product needed to remain clear of the existing underground railway system, which it does via an antlike maze of tunnels, stairwells, and elevator shafts.

Of course, the most important papers have already been collected and published, some of them many times.

ARCHIVIST ————————————————————————————

It may seem strange to you, but I never thought to ask him how he attained it. It was a gift, a wonderful gift, for me and for our family, and considering the difficulties of the years between the wars, it would have been terrible, unthinkable to question such unexpected good fortune. The previous tenants, I know nothing about them. They...

Disappeared?

Perhaps they wearied of the maintenance. I can't blame them!

Over coffee Herr Prinz showed me a map: a block away from the pension is an apartment building built on the site of the old Hotel Metropol, Gestapo headquarters, into whose basement his mother's lover, his father, an atheist and a musician, disappeared in 1941.

But as long as the scholars continue to parade through the city of Vienna, over, around, and through Herr Schönberg's various abodes and haunts, on their way toward the glamorous tragedy of the new Berlin, the sunshine and swimming pools of Schönberg's Los Angeles, it remains possible that an important bit of information may turn up here in this archive. One never tires of the search, the hunt for an answer, the key, the proof, as it were, of the hypothesis, and no doubt, somewhere in this archive there is a proof, perhaps several, to hypotheses past, present, and future.

Shadows, light, and dust. A scene Berg described as "the family misery of squalling children and bad-tempered old people." In the drawing room the ancient folk are sipping coffee. In another Charly and Steffi argue about a purchase while Erich wails unattended. Frau Berg comes bounding in, acknowledging Helene with a squeal. Hermann stumbles through a popular song on the piano (perhaps "Vera Violetta"—do you know it?). Smaragda and her girlfriend sit on a sofa together, stroking a large yellow cat. Children! Nannies! A great whirl of activity, do you see? But the camera never loses Helene. Is there some way to put a spotlight on her as she moves? Like a stage, a stage house, old and dusty, as in *Lulu*. She glides upstairs, finally, untouched by the squalor, and finds Alban in his room, on his bed, reading.

SOPRANO ⸻⸻⸻⸻⸻⸻⸻

Mix session for the electronic elements of "Mendel," the first part of an extended work of Walter's which he has yet to give even a provisional title. The score is a wild, multicolored collage of notational patterns, instructions, durational markings. Constructed in a Stockhausen-like statistical manner: layered microstructures derived from operations based in some way on Mendel's cross-breeding experiments. The control room buzzes with an electric hum, a frequency you feel more than hear, unfolding, percolating, revealing itself as a complex unity, a bundle of rhythms and tempos, all contained within the single tone that maintains a sort of stasis.

COMPOSER ⸻⸻⸻⸻⸻⸻⸻

Apart from owning cars, however, the numerous metal space-saving devices and larger, more obvious luxuries visible through the balcony windows of the apartment complex testify to the relative wealth of the flats' occupants.

ARCHIVIST ⸻⸻⸻⸻⸻⸻⸻

A servant calls his name, and he holds out his hand to Helene. The servant disappears. Helene holds out the laurel. They embrace. The embrace evolves into a kiss and then fondling and exploration. Alban undoes her jacket and blouse, kisses her breasts. His hand moves between her legs. It will be awful and beautiful to see these young lovers in this environment. But then a figure passes in the foreground. Then another and another. You see?

But then the drone snaps, explodes into a profusion of looping, chattering, bubbling confetti, a hail of voices or the same voice, a storm of sound elements propagating exponentially into a new structure, much larger than the first, crushingly so, a shimmering wall of shifting amplitudes and frequencies, expanding faster and faster, beyond the range of quantifiable sensation. It suddenly shuts down with a crack.

More police on the streets these days. What are they anticipating? Panic? Elation?

Why not purchase a house or why not live closer to the First District, where most of the young men and women living in this complex work, in banks, in government offices, as doctors, lawyers, and tourism officials? Modernity. Youth. Social responsibility.

But the most important task, the first and most important, is to order the material, to archive it, to classify it, and record its existence.

Your uncle, he was known...
He was killed. In the last days of the war. Unfortunately. As I've said, those were the most tragic days. So. This is my favorite view in Vienna.

People are passing in the hall as Alban and Helene lower themselves to the floor. The traffic increases until the two are obscured and we see only a shifting foreground of dark forms. And then from this we transition to—what? I don't know. A train station? A busy street? Or perhaps an open space?

SOPRANO ————————————————————————————————

I have long been pleading that an hour should be given over to modern music, at a time when its opponents will not greatly begrudge it; for example, an hour late at night, once or twice a week, perhaps after eleven. That could be handed over to modern music with no envious reaction.

COMPOSER ————————————————————————————————

To the Archivist the complex seems like an immense steel hive, a commune with a school, a supermarket, an art gallery, a theater, a small, nondenominational place of worship. Each building has a committee and the committees have subcommittees, and the complex has a monthly congress and dinner. It was a government project.

ARCHIVIST ————————————————————————————————

The studio is already set up for a quartet arriving tomorrow to complete the recording.

Schönberg's claim on eleven o'clock, despite its ironic tone, seems an aberration for the polemicist, almost conciliatory in its concern for modern music's opponents. But it recalls us to the idea of education, its preeminence in the understanding of this music.

—How will you vote?
Even at home Wolf seems dressed for work. He is tall, tan, and blond. An educated proletarian. This is the image he wishes to convey. He is the hero of a science fiction novel.

Enter the Archivist. In socks and slippers, he stands in the doorway of his dim office. He pushes his glasses higher on the bridge of his thin, sharp nose and raises his coffee to his red lips. He blows on the coffee. He watches the violent ripples on the dark surface, the small drifting patches of foreign substances. Oil. Dust. He blows again on the coffee, then scans the cluttered room.

Perhaps we can get a picture of you there before we leave.
Oh, but not of me. It is the view, my dear. I particularly love it in the winter, you see. Look. Here. You see the church, there, and over there is where they have the Christmas market. It is unfortunate that we couldn't have done this then.

I am very interested in this idea of contrasting extremes that you have spoken about. Tell me what you think of this scene, but not by post, for God's sake! Why this insistence on the post, on mystery?
Yours—
Lotte Wallner

SOPRANO ——————————————————————————————

One of the engineers wants to talk politics with me during a break: Why do Americans believe everything the Jews tell them? Can't they see there's a conspiracy here, an attempt to discredit Austria and Waldheim? And who do you think's at the bottom of it? People should mind their own business and let Austrians do what's right for Austria.

After eleven, sliding through frequencies, after midnight, later, near and distant voices, German, Czech, English, murmuring to teenagers in the dark, young men and young women rotating through the city.

COMPOSER ——————————————————————————————

Wolf has good taste. He is a champion of radical art and free expression. His artistic awakening occurred in 1968, at Vienna University, when he watched the Actionist Gunter Brus, covered in his own shit, mutilate himself, drink his own piss, and masturbate while singing the national anthem. Wolf's political awakening occurred when Brus was arrested.

An American came by the archive today. The Russian is in the hall now. The American came by earlier.

ARCHIVIST ——————————————————————————————

Yes, the view is lovely. I like, there, at the far end, that little street. Where those buildings open up. The city seems to unfold there, doesn't it?
Yes, yes. But look how ugly it is now with all these election posters. That awful man.
Which one?

You won't remember will you, Alban? Alban—it is almost dawn and the early morning people have begun their work, opening the day, stoking the fires, rekindling—in the years after the war we could not care for our children.

American pop, debates about men and women, about war and radiation, about elections and the future, aliens, America, Zionism. All of this after eleven. After eleven the streets gradually empty. Vienna shuts the windows and doors, gets privately drunk, nods off in front of the television—documentaries, avalanches, slalom competitions. Static and American cops. Put on a little music, spin the dial to something a little more downbeat, something more sedate, sedated, sedating. Have another cup of coffee, tip your waiter, don't fall asleep with that cigarette burning. Lights flicker and then fail.

The apartment is spare and crystalline. Most of the furniture is glass, steel, or an amalgamation of the two. Even wooden objects are bleached to the point of unnatural whiteness. An ice cave. An antiseptic space vessel. The passive face of Dr. Steyrer stares in at them.

They were sick and starving, and we sent them to Switzerland with cards around their necks, like little parcels. The trains left every day, trainloads of underfed children. Lotte. A beautiful little blonde. In the Westbahnhof. I was on my way, I don't know where, a recital, a vacation. Peter was there, and there were hundreds of them, children waiting to be reclaimed by their parents. There was a woman wandering about calling for her daughter: Lotte. A beautiful little blonde tugged at the woman's sleeve. She was so pretty, with a new, black and white velvet dress, blonde curls, such a clean, sharp little face. Little Lotte.

SOPRANO ————————————————————————————————————

Am I a Jew? The engineer had been glaring at me since I arrived, making it apparent that now I was in the way, now I was disturbing one thing or another. I was not welcome. Almost from the moment of our introduction he's been grousing about Waldheim and Americans and Zionists and now he asks: Are you a Jew?

The red cabins of the Riesenrad sway and come to rest. After eleven. Buses, trams, taxis, isotopes, and something else on the move, too: information. Shadows on shadows. A poster goes up. Demonic horns sprout from the candidate's head. *Fairness for Waldheim!* The shadows scuttle away, wearing the shoes of Harry Lime. Hidden industry.

COMPOSER ————————————————————————————————————

Wolf, Maria, and their children are a modern family, an SPÖ family. Wolf is an official at the foreign ministry. Maria is the editor for a city weekly known for its progressive politics. Maria and Wolf speak of the future of Austria and the world as if they already lived there.

The Archivist hasn't seen the Russian for almost an hour, but he can hear him out there in the hall, blowing on the coffee the Archivist made for the two of them some time ago.

ARCHIVIST ————————————————————————————————————

Well, let's talk about something else.

I wanted to ask you about your favorite role.

Oh, but that is such a difficult question. As you know, I have played all the major roles in every language multiple times, and I have recorded them, most of them, at least once, so you see...

What is music today? In the minds of many, not what I nor what most of the musicians I know do. Not what Webern did. In fact, I feel as if the idea of New Music, music that people think of as being anticipated, enjoyed, music that was contemporary and reflected the current culture ceased being so-called "serious music" with Richard Strauss and Debussy.

The Archivist has discovered a hole in his sweater.

—How will I vote? Well. There's a question. I'm not certain. What would you like me to say, Wolf?

—The truth! Always the truth, of course!

Wolf's laugh echoes through the white apartment.

The coffee must be cold by now, but the Russian continues to blow on it out of habit. The Russian is doing research, he says, for a film about Alban Berg that he is producing with Lotte Wallner, the retired soprano.

Yes, well, what I meant was—I wanted to ask you what your destiny role was, your Shicksals-role. *Whether you enjoyed it or not, the role you feel you were meant to play. Was it Tosca, a role you played to great acclaim so many times, or Sieglinde, a role from very early in your career?*

But her mother kept pushing her away. *Stop it, you! I want my little girl! Lotte! Lotte!* But you won't remember this, Alban, you cannot know how things were then. Lotte. Lotte. A beautiful little blonde.

SOPRANO ————————————————————————————

Since then we have only an endless rearrangement of Western music's traditional elements. We're shuttling back and forth through a closed system, a complete and objective reality embodied by the parameters set by music stores around the world. The art song gives way to the pop lyric.

COMPOSER ————————————————————————————

Maria enters from the kitchen with a decanter of wine and a glass for herself. Sunlight and hidden lights, hidden in the ceiling, in the walls, in the wine. The decanter throws a scarlet polygon of light on the white carpet.

ARCHIVIST ————————————————————————————

Yes, the thing about that role—though I will say first that it is not the answer to your question—Sieglinde was the only Wagner role I played for the first decade of my career, though I was asked several times to play Brünhilde quite early on. But I knew that would be a disaster, you see. I was too young. I had had a terrible experience earlier, in Rome, and I knew this would go as badly or even worse, so I refused. A few days later, I received a letter from Hitler, in his handwriting, signed by him—I still have it—asking me again to play Brünhilde in Berlin, but I turned it down again.

We're alone in the hall during a break. I've done little to check the engineer's onslaught. There's too much work to be done in the studio for me to contradict him and stir up a real dogfight. I don't want to be a distraction to Walter. I nod. I grunt. I shrug.

Now jazz and rock, they have their own histories and have passed through stages of development resembling those of serious music, though much faster, being at once alternate branches of the original stalk and its progeny, so that in some sense, while musical, technical, and cultural forces unique to each have shaped their development, they have, as well, learned from and retraced, or at least mimicked, the historical developments of so-called serious music.

—Sunday, Maria says, sighing. At least we'll be done with the subject.
—Oh, I think you'll never be done with politics. Will she, Wolf?

In the summer of 1945, Russian troops stabled their horses in the most popular Viennese cafés. Before the war, the Archivist's father spent many hours at the Café Central playing chess, and he continued to do so during the few times he was home on leave from Mauthausen.

I have trouble following the engineer's rapid, colloquial speech. And then a question I understand: Am I Jew? He is no thug, this engineer, no Hun. A slim and angular man. Short silver hair and fashionable horn-rimmed glasses. An intelligent, professional technician. Not someone to fear. And I feel no fear.

And now, perhaps more than ever, these different forms of music, as well as innumerable others, different genres, seem to exert an equal amount of influence on each other.

COMPOSER

Maria refills their glasses.
—Prost!
—I was thinking of voting Green, actually.
A frighteningly explosive laugh erupts from Wolf's well-toned depths. He lurches forward, as if about to vomit.

The Archivist's father was also an archivist. The Archivist's father took great pleasure in discovering and discussing the complexities of chess, as though some part of his mind itself was an archive of the game's history, of gambits and endgames, to which he added material ceaselessly, voraciously. And later? Perhaps desperately.

ARCHIVIST

Peter:

My darling. I'm sorry I've neglected you now for so long. Really, I do feel awful about it, awful as I haven't for so many years. I know it is ridiculous, love, but listen to me again, now, hear me again. Who knows if this won't be the last time, if something might happen and I am unable to ever write again? Ah, I hear you cajoling me out of my little melodrama. Have a drink with me? Yes, drink, drink, drink with me. For me.

Where are you, Peter? What are you doing tonight and who are you with? Or are you asleep? Have you taken to early nights? Yes, I think you may have. I think so.

SOPRANO ——

I feel sick. I feel foolish. Stunned. And this makes me sick, embarrassed by my lack of speech. I don't answer, and the engineer lets his question hang. Am I a Jew? It is both a question and a deduction. It is a conclusion, for him, easily reached. And I have made it easier by my silence. Webern was a Jew. Musically, at least, and from a Nazi perspective, though the genealogy he produced proves, as it was meant to, otherwise. Yet perhaps one might accept Webern as a Jew despite himself, accept him as one in that era who suffered, who was silenced. The double of this other, Aryan Webern. Through this twisted mirror, through this perverse notion of solidarism, the engineer's perverse question is turned on its head.

COMPOSER ——

The Archivist himself never took much interest in chess, nor in any game. For him the usefulness of games had always been limited to the information one gleaned about others by watching them at play.

ARCHIVIST ——

Well, you know Hitler kept after me, he would not be refused, and I received a request from him the following year to play Elsa. I talked it over for a few days with Peter, my husband at the time, and with his help I found the courage to accept.

What year was that?

It must have been late 1940 or early 1941.

How did you feel knowing that your appearance was endorsed by the Nazi regime?

I think it is rather difficult to explain today how things were in Austria in those days, and Germany, too, of course, difficult to describe and to be understood. So much has been written and said, so much time has passed that even the people who were there and who lived through that time, good people, people who have nothing to be ashamed of, seem to have forgotten how we lived.

So then: You are asleep, and I am whispering in your ear, writing these foolish words and letting them slide down the page into your ear, into your silent mind, and then where? Perhaps to mingle with all your numbers, your accounts, your figures, your bills and assets and secret codes. Your private ledgers.

SOPRANO ————————————————————————————————

The engineer lets the question hang, and so do I. He shows no discomfort. I feel no fear. Am I? I am not fearful of him, but I still feel sick at the thought of my ill-preparedness. Unguarded, unmindful of the power of the true believer. Unwary in a moment, my moment, abundant with specters.

COMPOSER ————————————————————————————————

An archive is a bit of infinity. This is what the Archivist tries to explain to the American when they are standing in the hall, when the American has completed his search. A brief search, and he, the American, seems dissatisfied. The Archivist feels the need to explain. What? He feels the need to explain the nature of the archive. Why? So that the place of his own archive in the overall continuum of archiving activity (human, biologic, geologic, cosmic, etc.) will become apparent.

ARCHIVIST ————————————————————————————————

Yes, yes, there was a lot of violence. Violence against Jews. And against others. Against Austrians, too. But I think I know more about that now than I or many other people did at the time.

Darling, why Berlin? You never liked the place and now, forever, never come back, never anymore, my Peter. Are you dead? And will I know if you are? Will someone telephone in the middle of the night? And who will this woman be?

What is of interest here is the way in which that branch of musical endeavor generally referred to as the avant-garde—encompassing composers from Webern to Cage, et al.—has become increasingly isolated, despite its development of new arrangements of new materials, its incorporation of not only new instruments but new technologies, its continued curiosity about the nature and meaning of both sound and hearing.

The American is not the first to leave disappointed. The Archivist hates to make explanations. He despises the need he sometimes feels to make them, particularly to dissatisfied Americans, yet he cannot prevent himself from doing so. An archive is a bit of infinity.

And if you think about the violence that we lived through, particularly in Vienna, during the period between the wars, you can see that what we did see or know about early on—I must emphasize that, early on—was merely an act of a state trying to create the kind of order we all wanted, that we had not had since the previous century.

In his memoir, Reverberations, *Dietrich Fischer-Dieskau says that there was no way, as time went by, that one could not have known what was happening to the Jews.*

SOPRANO ⸻

What is the meaning of this isolation? Is there a musical avant-garde? Is there any need for one?

COMPOSER ⸻

An archive is an attempt to preserve what is important, what is valuable, to distill these things out of the general flow of the products of existence. This space, the space of the archive (that is, the imagined realm where all archived material can be accessed) is infinite but not unchanging. Additions, deletions, and alterations of the character of the specific areas occur frequently.

ARCHIVIST ⸻

Yes, but he also acknowledges having interpreted what he saw in those days retroactively. In any case, that is true of the later days, but I am talking about the early years, before the war. No one knew what was coming in 1931, believe me. No one knew. And in these days—1940, 1941—no one wanted to know. People were proud and, I don't know, perhaps they were a little frightened. They wanted to reap the benefits of a strong nation, and they were afraid, maybe without understanding why, that if they protested, if they spoke a little too loudly, these benefits would come to an end.

No. When serious music becomes an objective entity (as it has) the concept of extension via avant-gardism dies. So the avant-garde itself, having no other direct developmental influence except on itself, becomes its own category, its own strange and separate species.

The archive, this one and any other, is a greater entity than any of the individuals who visit it.

I think later, particularly after Stalingrad, these same people, for the same reasons, were just as frightened of the end of the war. They realized, as you say, what was going on, and they knew they could live without Hitler, but the problem of the end was the same as before: his exit would be the end of the good life again, of order and prosperity.

I think many people would find that idea of prosperity a bit difficult to understand.

Well, this is just my opinion, as I see it, having been there at the time.

SOPRANO ————————————————————————————

Experimental musicians conduct research in the art of sound production and arrangement, the art of communicating ideas through sound, i.e., composition. A mission not different in its general directive from Beethoven's.

COMPOSER ————————————————————————————

Wolf tries to catch the wine dripping from his nose and lips in his free hand. But there is wine on the carpet. Maria glides away. —Green? Really? You'll have plenty of company, I suppose, with this accident in the Ukraine. This wine really is shit, isn't it? I'll tell Maria to open a different bottle.

ARCHIVIST ————————————————————————————

That is what I mean about being understood. People are more sensitive to these issues now, of course, but at the time, in Vienna and elsewhere, too, prosperity and safety were things you cherished above all else.

They came to interview me today, Peter. An American magazine, checking up on me, hounding me. Just checking to see if I still breathe, if I still live.

What is different, then, is the specific product, what is heard, what is seen, what is given to the performer. And yet, in my mind, this product, say Cage's *Fontana Mix*, or Lincoln's *Ganymede*, or my trio, is no different in its general intent than the *Eroica*, these works no less identifiable as musical productions. In fact, these particular works—mine, Cage's, Lincoln's—all attempt to expand the definition of what music is, well beyond both the parameters that dictated the composition of the *Eroica* and those of subsequent works.

The children blow into the apartment, laughing and shouting at the end of a footrace, Rosa the winner.
—What're you cooking, Mama?
—Hello, Uncle!
—Hello, Uncle!
—Hello, girls. Who is the champion?
—I am!
Rosa smiles, victorious, and receives a kiss from the Archivist, her uncle.

You can see it still, though Americans never seem to recognize it for what it is. I mean, in general, the aspects of European cities that appear cosmopolitan to Americans are those that most resemble something in their own cities.

All the old questions, the questions they have always wanted to ask, but you wouldn't let them. Do you remember, Peter? The ones they would not have dared to ask: What did you think of this? How did you feel about that? Where were you? Where were you? Where were you?

SOPRANO ─────────────────────────────────────

(Though, of course, these same parameters have no bearing on Beethoven's instinct for sound production as a form of expression, no bearing on his individual decisions about what sounded good.

COMPOSER ─────────────────────────────────────

Marta also receives a kiss and a consoling pat on the head. But she pouts a little nevertheless.

ARCHIVIST ─────────────────────────────────────

Everything else, the slow and sometimes guarded manner of shopkeepers, the careful management of utilities, the economy of spaces, all these things that are foreign to the American way of thinking are portrayed in that country as a sort of comical and antiquated form of stage business.

There is no telling, for instance, what Beethoven might have produced had he lived in our era of tapes, electronics, and indeterminacy. The age, the taste and technology of the age determine the articulation of the composer's instinct, but not the tendencies, the affinities of the instinct itself.)

—We tied.
—No we didn't! I won by my big toe.
Rosa receives another kiss. This one from her father.
—Don't crow, Rosa. Let it be and go play a noncompetitive game with your sister.
—When can we eat?
—Soon, dear, Maria says, returning with another bottle of wine.

I don't know the answers anymore, Peter. I cannot answer. Must answer. We all must be truthful, mustn't we, Peter? But why now Berlin? Why, damn you?

SOPRANO ──────────────────────────────────────

It's the kind of thing one experiences in autumn or spring in cities like Vienna, so dependent on light and shadow, mirrors and reflectivity, when the air is clear and in transition: how a change in light can alter a city's psyche and cause certain colors to seem more relevant. There's a shade of scarlet on the Ringstraße that I've sensed for days but only really noticed today in the presence of the May Day reds. They're everywhere, on walls, at tramstops, on kiosks: announcements of the imminent arrival of the Dalai Lama. He will speak at the Industriellen Vereinigung.

COMPOSER ──────────────────────────────────────

—Supper will be ready by the time you change your clothes and wash your face.
But the two girls go outside onto the balcony to water the plants and watch the sunset. Rosa asks her sister the names of build-ings as she points to them, across the river.

ARCHIVIST ──────────────────────────────────────

But these mannerisms that I believe I harbor as much as the grocer on the corner—don't forget that despite my family's historical wealth I grew up in very humble circumstances—these mannerisms have developed out of these times we have been discussing, times of turmoil and want, when you did not know whether what you or your family had established would be worth anything from one week to the next.

Spring is the season for luminaries: the Prince and Princess of Wales, Chancellor Kohl, His Celestial Holiness, Russian cesium.

It's not unreasonable today to identify the current set of these parameters as the Market, not unreasonable to identify any set this way for any age, accepting that its human agents have always been identifiable as such, regardless of the ways in which their social relationship to the artist has changed over time.

Wolf watches his daughters and sips his wine.
—They're always talking about you, Maria says to the Archivist, her brother. They want to come and stay with you for a weekend. They think it will be a great adventure. And they want to ride the train by themselves.

The Archivist was tired and hungry. His father had stopped talking, and the Archivist had begun to hate the man and his responsibility for the turn all their lives had taken. He was glad, finally, to be free of him.

I'm certain we could go on at some length about this subject, but I'm equally certain my editor would prefer that we to return to music.
Of course, I am sorry. What were we talking about?
Your destiny. The role you were destined to play.

And what am I supposed to tell them: my life, our lives were music? We weren't there. We weren't anywhere. We were on stage. Only there. I wasn't me. I wasn't anyone but a character, an aria.
SOPRANO ───

The Market, then, not the artist, designates the boundaries between genres, generates a sort of Linnaen system of classification where certain branches clearly end in genetic isolation and extinction. Isolation seems to be the current situation of so-called experimental music.
COMPOSER ───

But the Archivist lied when he arrived at the family's appointed meeting place and found that only his uncle, his mother, and his sister, Maria, had survived. He told them he had buried his father in a patch of grass overlooking a valley with a small, still lake reflecting the mountains and the clear blue sky.
ARCHIVIST ───

I was a voice. Isn't that the truth? Isn't that the way it was? You were there with me, Peter. You know the truth. You can tell what happened. You were always so good at telling. We were a voice, and the voice was asked to do things, and the voice performed as it had to. Isn't that right?

What's particularly interesting about this, however, is the difference between my own experience, the experience of my generation, and Webern's—his a period of transition, the node from which a new stem, our stem, sprouted—the difference between our relationships with critics and audiences, with the history and future of music.

—A visit would be fine. The weather is good now for a ramble. Up to the Kahlenberg. Would they like that?
—I'm sure, Maria says.

And now you are not here. You won't protect me anymore. I am only a body now, darling, old and quiet, but they haven't forgotten. Not quite. A collector's item. An old stamp from far away. An old bone the hounds are set to dig up. Is it wrong for me to feel hunted? Is that going too far? Perhaps. It is only one girl. One interview.

SOPRANO ————————————————————————————

The theoretical and experimental worlds we inhabit, those seeds that finally flowered after the war, are Webern's legacy. With the war's significant influence on our development, however, on the development of every human endeavor, every vice, perhaps we feel less that weight of responsibility to history. Perhaps one can feel less responsibility altogether, can settle into a life of art, of quiet investigation, quiet production.

COMPOSER ————————————————————————————

The Archivist sometimes dreams about his father, and for years he thought he recognized him in the streets of Vienna: an old man walking with a cane, counting his steps, buying a newspaper, counting vowels, leaving a locksmith's shop, riding a bicycle, counting keys, rotations. And then at night, always at night, particularly after it had rained, the lingering shadow walked the streets, his footsteps distinct in the Archivist's ears, and his whispered numbers mounted vertiginously. But there was no one. A dog. A fleeing shadow.

ARCHIVIST ————————————————————————————

Yes, my *Shicksals*-role. Yes, well, actually I was just getting to that because I was telling you that I was requested to sing *Lohengrin*...
By Hitler.
In Berlin, *Lohengrin*, Elsa, and that, in fact, is the answer to your question.

She asked about *Lohengrin*, about Elsa, about the first time. She asked about the child, Peter. I could not believe it. She seemed just about to leave and then this question, the most horrible, the most tasteless. The photographer had gone to lunch. And you were not here. There was no one to say, "That is enough! Out!"

Lotte Wallner was the clear monarch of the evening, even in retirement, even amid the rarefied and spangled array of Viennese celebrity; her perfect voice was intimate in the overheated room.

Wolf laughs.
—Yes! Take them up the Kahlenberg, tire them out! They don't get enough exercise around here, except running up and down the stairs, late for school. Your sister lets them sleep too late.
Wolf's tendency to criticize Maria, even to blame her for minor incidents or complications that are either Wolf's fault or blameless, has often annoyed the Archivist, though he has never brought it up with his sister. She herself seems not to notice.

Yes, I see. Elsa is one of the roles you've performed most frequently and certainly is the most recorded. What has made her so important to you?

Well, many sopranos find her difficult or at least undesirable simply because they cannot muster any sympathy for her.

I lied. Peter, I lied as I did on stage. And I laughed. Only you would have recognized my falseness. No one else is alive or sane enough to remember. I was wonderful. I was wonderful again.

SOPRANO ——————————————————————————————————————

Of course, her program was relatively short and had obviously been planned to avoid too much strain on her voice. A bit of Schubert and Brahms, ending with a couple of love songs to Vienna, accompanied by the host on accordion.

COMPOSER ——————————————————————————————————————

—We've promised them a ski trip next season, Wolf says. Maybe you'll come with us this time.
—Yes, says the Archivist. Maybe.
Maria pours more wine.

ARCHIVIST ——————————————————————————————————————

But you've always been able to do this, even to play the role differently throughout your career.

Yes, my Elsa evolved as I evolved as a singer. In those first performances in Berlin, she was what one might call starstruck, as was I. And this attitude worked for me for many reasons, perhaps most of all because I was so young. Elsa's simplicity, her innocence, were apparent in my own face.

Is this a reproach? Am I making accusations that we swore never to make, you and I? Yes, I do remember.

The pianist was exceptional, the more so, I think, because he's a dental surgeon by trade. An intelligent and very musical man, but he told me, and being in the same boat myself (that is, being a guest of Walter and his wife), I knew, he wouldn't have been invited had he not been Lotte Wallner's accompanist.

Rosa embraces her sister. They sing a song about the woods.
—They do take good care of each other, don't they?
—Yes, Maria says. Yes.

SOPRANO ――――――――――――――――――――――――――――――――――

And the guest list was remarkable: leading actors from the
Burgtheater, a film producer, the pop star Falco, a journalist writing
a book about the children of Nazis, all the high-ranking SPÖ
officials. Kurt Steyrer himself directed me to the toilet, a wretched
little closet stowed between floors. Still, the palace was grand, a
magic box, constructed of smaller gilt and marble magic boxes.

COMPOSER ―――――――――――――――――――――――――――――――――

Maria looks at her watch and then toward the kitchen. She twists
her wedding ring.
—Rosa, help Marta wash up for supper.
Rosa whispers in her sister's ear, and the two go rushing through
the house, down the hall. A door slams. Wolf and his family
usually eat at the same time every day. But tonight the prepara-
tions are taking a bit longer. And the Archivist arrived late. Wolf
studies the Archivist.

ARCHIVIST ―――――――――――――――――――――――――――――――――

If I accuse, I accuse us both, as it was and always will be for me. Both together. Partners in sacrifice. Every one of us was so caught up in their sacrifice. Didn't we keep records of it in ledgers, carry it with us in our pocketbooks? And now there is too much bitterness, Peter, too much darkness to pour into your ears. You might never wake, and that would be all the worse. Write to me. Come to me. Return.

Ever—

Lotte

Is that what I meant to say, that we are freer today? That we, creators of artifacts, of representations and theories, aesthetics and abstractions, are enjoying an era of *less* responsibility? The same weightlessness, the same remove, the same ill-prepared-ness that clouded Webern's already myopic vision in 1933, when the proscription of his music in Germany was, as he implied, only part of a program of "changes in artistic production," when the Nazi regime must surely be as finite as any republic he'd known, when fascism was merely a matter of aesthetic differ-ence, a redefinition of art?

The archive will remain unchanged by the visit of the American. It, like all archives, is a field on which scholars graze medita-tively but which nonetheless never surrenders a single shoot. So, then, is this scholarly mastication an illusion? Whose? The scholar's? But he produces a book, which may in its turn also be archived. The archive's? But that would imply a certain sentience on the part of this immobile, inanimate (yet organic) entity that would defy reason, the basis of archiving activity.

Everything about those first performances, even the smallest gestures, was kept simple and trembling. That audience wanted to see a rather wrathful Lohengrin, powerful, imposing, coming to rescue not only Elsa, the pure, helpless visionary, the threatened maiden, but also this historical, historically threatened Germany.

And Alban, what about the child, Lotte? Lotte, the little girl who never was? Mine, Peter's, Lotte poisoned in the womb. And me left with no one now? It was important to me, to us, for me to perform. It was important, yes, more important than anything, that I perform in Berlin when I had the chance. And it was spectacular. There was not time enough in that world for delay.

SOPRANO ————————————————————————————————————

They don't look up much, the Viennese, but from time to time they do see me, in my office, a visitor in a cold, high-ceilinged cave. My study. My wilderness. Perhaps they feel an unfamiliar prick, a communication of life from above where normally there's only decoration. Ornament.

Theories. Too many theories. More revelations, more questions, more theories about what happened, when, who was responsible, why. Can a catastrophe stand such analysis? Is analysis proper in Waldheim's case, when condemnation is required, unquestioning, exemplary condemnation?

COMPOSER ————————————————————————————————————

—I can tell you're a Waldheim man because you won't answer me directly!
—Wolf, Maria says. Not so loud. Can we please talk about something else? Don't bully him.

(That is to say, archiving is an atavistic activity, engaged in by the inanimate as well as by the sentient, at which point it becomes a practice, as opposed to the product of insensate forces working in conjunction or opposition.)

ARCHIVIST ————————————————————————————————————

He was to overwhelm us with divine martial virtue, you see, save us from unholy pagan magic and the scourge from the east. But the times change, of course, to say the least, yes? After the war was a time of questions, doubt, accusations, denials.

This is what we agreed. We could not let her live. I bore Elsa instead. But I was sick every night, Alban, every night between acts and all night long and all morning because of my uncle and his potions and alchemy. The butcher. I was too strong, too strong for any of it, but it killed me anyway, didn't it, killed Lotte and everything?

Is defense a crime? How essential is precise documentation at the extremities of crime? To have known and not acted. Nothing more should be said. One motive producing many crimes, different in kind, but finally motive is the issue, indefensible, and this must be felt, must be enforced, before science and evidence and theory begin their seductions.

—Hush, darling, Wolf says, taking a loud sip from his wine glass. A thump down the hall.
—Go check on the girls, won't you? Darling?
Maria says nothing.
—Well, I can't say for sure, says the Archivist.
—Tell us more about your visitors, Maria says.

The younger directors wanted a stronger Elsa, one with more sense and, ultimately, passion. I had matured enough to understand and explore her in this way.

Your singing became somewhat more erratic.

Yes, I suppose that is how many critics would put it, but for me it was simply a matter of humanity, bringing to my stage-world voices as I heard them in the street and in my own house. Old friends came to me and told me of their experiences, particularly at the hands of the Russians, terrible things.

SOPRANO ───────────────────────────────────────

Exile now before proof is offered, begging another round of questions. Isn't that right? A balance of passion and reason, yes, but the measure of the latter must decrease as we reach the extremities of criminality. Isn't that right? Isn't that instinctual, for the good of the species?

COMPOSER ───────────────────────────────────────

—What's that you say? Wolf asks.

—I said I can't say, the Archivist says. I don't know what to make of these accusations. There's a lot of talk. That's all.

No one moves. The girls laugh violently down the hall, behind their door.

ARCHIVIST ───────────────────────────────────────

At the beginning of the opera Elsa is falsely accused. She faces a penalty of death. I listened to my friends' tales of rape, incarceration, and torture, their troubled dreams, their hysterical reactions, and I tried to translate this for the stage.

I was ecstatic to learn that that man had been executed for his crimes. My uncle. Butcher, I said. I made Peter drink champagne with me, but you won't remember that, Alban. I smoked one of Peter's goddamned cigars and made him choke on the stench. It was the end. I blamed him. I blamed him, yes, but we killed me together; yes, we slaughtered Lotte and the whole lot of us. For Elsa.

Vienna is a city of faces. The buildings have faces. The façades have bodies, eyes, heads. But no movement, little movement. A rock of a city, the First District a canyon, sculpted, semiprecious, cold-blooded. It warms in the spring light.

The archive is changed by an archivist. He adds and disposes of what he sees fit, in accordance with not only the overarching mission of archiving, but also with the specific goals of the archive under his direction.

I played my Elsa as a damaged intelligence, gave her the hint of an intense and normal life before her murderous trials of soul and, finally, of the heart.

Rather like Ophelia, then?

Yes, absolutely. And think of it: What a world of fear and chaos, this kingdom that would give itself over so easily to a supernatural being, an eager warrior! Later it was impossible, impossible for my Elsa to be so trusting.

SOPRANO ————————————————————————————————

An aesthetic canyon, authenticated on nearly every block with the watermark of perfection, idealism in the arts, a German trademark cribbed from the Greeks: the Greek key. It's everywhere, inside and out.

The particles circulate expansively:

Cs 134	Nb 95	Te 132
Cs 136	Mo 99	La 140
Cs 137	Ru 103	Np 239
Ba 140	I 131	Cm 141
Zr 95	I 133	Cm 144

COMPOSER ————————————————————————————————

—I know what to make of them, Maria says.

—Sit down, darling.

In this way a particular archivist may alter the character of an archive, especially if he has been given the power to make amendments to the goals of his archive. In this way an archivist may reshape an archive so that it more closely resembles himself and his own interest in the subject at hand.

ARCHIVIST ————————————————————————————————

I constructed a weltanschauung around Elsa's doubt. Not the naif's distrust, the flower of Ortrud's schemes, of a political rival's manipulations, but the deeper skepticism of a young woman. Elsa's nature is noble, imperial. At her center is doubt, or rather refusal. Through her trials, her natural nobility emerges in the manner of a butterfly.

M. Cholodenko—
Another scene for you to review: the first meeting. 1911. A plush red parlor in the Innere Stadt. Young men and ladies, observed by older women. The youths argue points of literature and music. We see her hand, slim, long-fingered, poised like a statue's.

The Greek key. An endlessly repeating, interlocking pattern of right angles. And when you turn your head and spot it out of the corner of your eye, you can't help thinking for a moment that this simple, repeating, crosslike design reminds you of another one.

—Sit down, please.
Wolf points to Maria's chair.
—He's a criminal.
—Well, says the Archivist.
—A criminal!
—Yes, one could certainly make that case. But not so big a criminal as some. He was not a leader. He issued no orders.
Wolf laughs his explosive laugh.
—I knew it! I knew you were for him!

SOPRANO

And the faces. They don't give individual buildings character so much as they do the city, this district. Men, women, beasts, gods, wooing, weeping, blissful, asleep, agog, glaring, but most of all unvigilant.

COMPOSER

—I'm not. Not necessarily. I'm trying to make a distinction.
—Why? Maria demands, her voice growing shrill. What's the point in that? A distinction. A distinction about what? Levels of criminality? A criminal like that is only ever a criminal.

ARCHIVIST

This is the blossoming of the intelligence I spoke of. Alone with him in the bedchamber in Act Three, Elsa is a woman, but not because she is a wife, not in anticipation of the wedding night. Perhaps those are the expectations one brings to the theater. Oh, what a silly girl! So easily swayed! She is ruining everything! But why should we trust Lohengrin? Elsa's is the skepticism of the mortal world, our world—even in the opera house—a necessary refusal, a demand for answers that exposes Lohengrin, rather, as the sort of holy fool Wagner would return to in *Siegfried* and *Parsifal*. These are vital operas, yes, but I never cared for those men, so laden with higher purposes in which love, human love, plays no part, none at all.

The gargoyles and guardians are designed to ward off baseness, imperfection, and filth. They gaze down on you with the intensity of Rilke's torso of Apollo, but disingenuously, cynically, disconnected as any forgery from the transformative power of the sincere.

Of course, such alterations in an archive are never permanent. Though some aspects of an archivist's work may survive for quite a long time, an archivist's impositions on his archive (a natural impulse, to be sure, and one which, when not careless, is certainly above rebuke) are never more permanent than the archive itself, the idea of the archive, the collection of thoughts, deeds, and artifacts, for example, of Arnold Schönberg.

Wagner, I think, knew this intuitively in his wavering over the opera's ending. Lohengrin's unnatural expectations are finally too burdensome. To be untainted by doubt? One cannot love under such conditions, cannot be human. He is a magical concoction after all. It is perfectly natural that Wagner should have wanted them to ascend into the heavens together, like Faust and Gretchen, I suppose, Elsa the penitent. Such things may have been possible to imagine in Goethe's age, but Wagner was a beginning to our century. With Wagner even the gods are corrupt. Truthfully, they should have remained so. An age of necessary doubt, you see. Noble refusal. Elsa remains behind, a victim, perhaps, but victorious too, even in her death, her mortality.

SOPRANO ───────────────────────────────────────

The stone gods gaze out over the city, elevated to an unattainable domain, ignoring as best they can the faceless Hofs of Leopoldstadt: brown stucco headstones blocking the sunrise.

COMPOSER ──────────────────────────────────────

—What do you mean, "like that"?
—And I don't want a criminal to represent my country. Never again!
—You know what she means. People want to stand up for their country. Yes! To be proud Austrians. Good! And they don't want to be told what to do, how to vote, how to think. But they're not listening to the facts!

ARCHIVIST ──────────────────────────────────────

As I say, I adopted for myself a similar natural and imperial right to refuse, and therefore to govern, and met with my own disasters. *The end of your relationship with Peter Litschauer.*
Yes. And another marriage. All the various feuds, yes. Peter was the most difficult for me. But my career remained strong and, you know, it was all mine until the end.

Another hand offers a glass of wine, and she fingers the stem thoughtfully before accepting. We see her face, Helene Nahwoski, and his, too, and he starts to introduce himself: "I am Maria's brother, Alban." And she teases him: "Maria's little brother, little Alban." And you know it goes on like this, very simple, very harmless.

Am I unfair? I am.

—Facts. What facts? No one has proven a thing. The Jewish Congress says he knew about deportations, and Waldheim says he didn't. Who do you expect people to believe?
—And that is another thing: You know there are people all over this city, Jewish people, receiving letters and phone calls threatening them, their families, their homes, their businesses. Doesn't that concern you?

But you must communicate their passion, you see, already there. Youthful passion, curiosity in the case of Berg because then we can pit this vigorous boy, witty boy, against his body. Very sad.

SOPRANO ————————————————————————————————

In letters to his wife Alban Berg used numerous pet names for both himself and Helene. Signed off sometimes with his musical initials:

A minor second. And Webern? His signature? The magic square?

Today is a useless day: the shops are too full of people buying and selling, and nothing at all has happened in Austria, nothing that the whole country should or would care about.

COMPOSER ————————————————————————————————

—Yes, of course, that is terrible and very stupid, but if every man in Waldheim's situation were to step aside because of such things, because someone said he had been a Nazi, there would be very few men in office today.

The mountains above Innsbruck were beautiful, were terrible during the summer of 1945.

ARCHIVIST ————————————————————————————————

And also during this party we see another boy with whom Helene has become infatuated, Raoul. The scene ends on the street: the group, surrounded by shadows, chattering away, saying good night, getting into their cabs or walking home. Helene is riding home to Hietzing with Raoul and two other young ladies. But she offers Alban her hand to kiss. All this happens very quickly and in the midst of a whirl of farewells, but we miss nothing, do you see? Come to me soon, please, and tell me your thoughts. Lotte Wallner

---

Letters are in the mail, protests are being planned, petitions and proposals lie unread on government desks. It is Thursday, of course.

—You're oversimplifying.
—I'm saying we've lived through very difficult times.
—Oh, I don't understand all this. What are you talking about?
—I'm saying we've lived through difficult times and that people like Waldheim made choices we would all prefer they hadn't made. But that's history, thank God.
—History. History? And all should be forgiven?

You mentioned the beginning of our century a moment ago, and I'd like to hear more on your relationship to modern music.
Well, you must keep in mind the time in which I was raised and in which I received my musical training. Berg, Schönberg, and Webern really were at the farthest edge of contemporary music.

My dearest little Lotte:
Again I return to conjure you in the middle of the night like a fearsome old crone whispering spells over your tomb—after midnight tonight, the first of May, the Night of Unrest. And stolen maypoles.

SOPRANO ——————————————————————————

The small archive wasn't particularly useful, being concerned mostly with the task of preserving materials having to do with Schönberg. I wonder what Webern would have felt to have seen such a thing, to see his relatively small, subordinate role in this particular memory of his mentor's, his friend's life.

The shifting winds make it unlikely now, less likely that we'll be poisoned by Soviet isotopes. It has become a perfect day, then, a glorious day for Vienna, on which nothing very serious will occur.

COMPOSER ——————————————————————————

—Wolf. It was forty years ago. More.
—You're not going to say "a man can change," I hope.
—Well.
Maria laughs.
—Change. Of course, let him change, then. Let him do it in prison.
—Oh yes, at Spandau. Or why not in Israel, at the end of a rope, like Eichmann?

The alps lay quiet in the sun: no skiers, no climbers. Only at sundown: the shadows of the refugees, the fugitives, the resisters haunted the roads, scuttling from haystack to cottage to cave to wood.

ARCHIVIST ——————————————————————————

During much of the first part of my career their music was banned, so you can imagine how stifling that can be in the early going. Of course, I am not trying to imply a lack of appreciation for the standard repertoire, even without that portion of it that was banned by the National Socialists. But I always envied, in a way, those younger singers who were better prepared for the postwar music than I was.

I dreamt you standing on the train. That was all. I had no way of knowing where you were going. I could hardly see you through the grumbling crowd.

And that's it, isn't it? The archive as a panorama of the life and times. This one was a bit limited as yet, but the archivist has big plans for expansion, it seems.

There were secret murders at night in the bowels of forgotten canyons, and then that guilty silence would be broken by the barking of a dog, scattered gunfire, a brief scream. The mountains were the most dangerous then because they were the last place on earth.

Of course, you knew there was new music being made outside of Germany, but you had no access, or only limited access, and if you didn't understand it you had nobody to ask about it. Now imagine, after nearly a decade, emerging into this world of Darmstadt and electronic music. Well, it took some time, of course, before all that really got started, but there was a continuing dialogue going on about music all that time, and as a performer essentially bound to German territories I was cut out of that conversation. Nevertheless, I am quite proud of having been involved with several early postwar stagings of Berg's operas and Schönberg's, as well as performances of Cerha's completed *Lulu*.

SOPRANO ————————————————————

A glorious day in May. Are there people suffering, ill, aging, destitute? Can it be on such a day as this? Are there people starving in the streets of a town or city, in their miserable hovel in this very country? People in prison? Has someone died? A plot, a murder? Was someone assaulted? Go into the forest. Find a high perch and look down over the valley. Go to the park. Think of nothing. Do not ruin this day.

COMPOSER ————————————————————

The Archivist and his father had been separated from the Archivist's mother and two sisters after the fall of Vienna, but the family had made a plan for such an eventuality. They would reunite at his uncle's house in Zell am See. On the road, the Archivist and his father had encountered an old companion of the father from Mauthausen who convinced them to flee into the mountains instead. He told them that the Russians would surely shoot them if they were captured, in or out of uniform.

ARCHIVIST ————————————————————

And now, as I understand it, you're getting into film?
Yes.
This is a work about Alban Berg. Is it a documentary?
Oh, no, no. It is going to be a drama, a love story, really, based on the collected letters.
How far along is the project?
Well, I have a director, Mikhail Cholodenko, but I am just sketching out scenes at the moment. Who knows whether it will come to anything? Of course, I generally live without deadlines now, and I love it, so I won't venture a guess at a premiere date.
Of course. Do you have time for a final question?
Of course!

The archivist himself was an interesting character. Gave me a brief lecture on his understanding of the business of archiving. "An archive is a bit of infinity," he said. A very serious man, thin, pale, a musician, too, I think. He had a number of scores on his desk that he'd obviously been studying, making performance notes in.

—Yes! And why not? Perhaps he should have been hung with the rest of them!
They sit in silence.
—You mean to say, the Archivist begins, that if your father...
—Your father, too.
—Our father were the monster at the end of the rope...
—Our father killed no Jews, no gypsies, no women and children. He experimented on no one. Sterilized no one. He issued no orders. Our father was not a criminal.

The windows were dark as if we were in a tunnel, and the dim lights flickered unsteadily. Did you see me? Someone reached out to you, and you turned before the lights went out again. I saw the curve of your lips that could have meant either pleasure or revulsion. Will you ride that train to me and fill me with the terror that is rightfully mine? Take as much of my sanity as will give you a form, dear. I would so like to hear your footsteps on my staircase every morning rather than the workmen's. Your accusations, your chemical smell rather than the labor and smoke of the city. We are alone, my sweet little darling. Will be alone. I think I could live for you now.

SOPRANO ————————————————————————————————————

The Webern house at Im Auholz 8 hasn't changed much from the time the family lived there. A sunroom's been added downstairs and a balcony, but the shed and the gazebo in the back garden are there as they were.

The matter of Webern, of course, is affirmation. The music is never dark after his shift to serialism. There is an optimism, a naive and romantic optimism even during the final year of the war, of his life, an illustration of his belief in science, the science of faith.

COMPOSER ————————————————————————————————————

—Yet you hate him all the same, says the Archivist.
—Don't you?
—Can I?
—You don't need my permission.
—Only if I wish to remember him as Papa.

For a time the Archivist and his father hid in the attic of a farmhouse. There were eight people living on the farm: a father and mother, their four boys, and the father's twin brother and his daughter. The youngest son brought them meals and told them when it was safe to come down. The Archivist understood that he and his father were a pleasant diversion.

ARCHIVIST ————————————————————————————————————

There is another role of sorts that matched, some might say sur-
passed, your Elsa in popularity. That is the multiple roles of the
grief-stricken parents of Mahler's Kindertotenlieder.
Yes. I see.
What was it that allowed you to inhabit these roles so completely?

The neighbor girl still lives next door. She remembers him as
quiet. He often stood in the doorway, smoking, she recalls. But
beyond this he seems to have had little contact with the neighborhood.

—You may remember our father any way you wish, but you
may never pardon him.
—Or myself, I suppose. I am as guilty as you, Maria.
—Not me.
—Those who failed to stop them, those who lived with them,
who loved them, before and after.
—Not me.
—You. You never loved Papa?
—He was a different man.
—He was the same man. Always the same.
Wolf fills their glasses with wine.
—And so then, he says, is Oberleutnant Waldheim.

The neighbor doesn't remember Webern's work in the garden, the garden he wrote so enthusiastically about to Josef Hueber— Hueber at the front, reading letters from his friend about the gentle struggles and victories of the garden at Im Auholz 8, praising the swift actions of the Wehrmacht. Hueber calls this Webern, the Webern of the garden, the *peasant* Webern.

Webern's science was a mixture of mysticism and botany, a mathematical formula, a new physics. His science is medieval in that it confirms God through the unfailing success of circular, unified complexities like the labyrinth, the journey, the pilgrimage to God, the pilgrim enlightened, retracing his steps, returning with God to his starting point.

COMPOSER

The Russian was in the hall. Now he is gone. He left without a word, leaving the Archivist to assume that he would return. But not today. It is too late, and the door to the archive is locked. The Archivist has gone, too. He is following the Russian.

They would relax in the parlor and tell the family of the world below. The peasant father and his brother said nothing. The boys asked about weapons. They asked what it was like to kill a man. They were convinced that the Archivist and his father— who had arrived in the middle of a moonless night—had stowed a small arsenal somewhere on the farm, perhaps in a haystack.

ARCHIVIST

I'm not sure what you mean. Inhabit? I feel a great affinity for Mahler's remarkable melodies, with the drama of his vocal works, of these songs in particular. They are, I think, his best.

Yes, perhaps inhabit *isn't...*
The right term. No. It is not.

Before the garden, before the peasant Webern, the little yard was home to geese and ducks and rabbits. The peasant Webern, the animals that preceded him, the silence of the house at the top of the hill are all still typical of the town today. Maria Enzersdorf remains a small market town on the outskirts of Vienna, on the edge of the forest. The heavy bombing, the Russian vehicles tearing through fences, the soldiers cutting boot soles from the leather of Webern's books, the alleged cache of weapons in the coal cellar are, as the neighbor says, history. *Geschichte*. Stories and tales.

The daughter was pretty, but she had affected a resigned look resembling her mother's, a look not uncommon to women in the mountains. She was mistreated by the four boys. The youngest would scald the backs of her knees with boiling water, and while she cried the older brothers would laugh and threaten to do their own mischief. "There is Austria," the Archivist's father whispered to his son in the hall. And at night, in the attic, the father whispered numbers.

This is a branch of history that leaves no trace, a dark fish returned to the primeval mud of a still, silver lake. "I live today for today," the neighbor says. And then she laughs, and the laugh is a prompt for me to laugh, too, to stop asking questions no one wants answered. Perhaps not even me.

At first the Archivist thought the numbers were a code, that his father was now a spy, that he had a little radio hidden in his coat. But they were only numbers. The father had been an archivist also. He had counted and recorded everything that had been brought to his office. Spectacles, for example. Suitcases. Shoes. Timepieces. Hairpieces. And now he simply counted, and the numbers grew larger and larger, into the millions, until he died. The Archivist searched his father's clothes then. He did not find a radio.

Then again, given your comments regarding Elsa, perhaps it is.
Is there a similar sense of refusal in your performance of these
songs? A refusal of death, perhaps? Of tragedy? Or of nihilism?
Perhaps.

I am certain of it. And once I have given you all of my attention,
won't we be reconciled? When you come, Lotte, we will not go
to the park. We will not go to the zoo and we will not go to the
museum. I am afraid there isn't time for that anymore. I am
afraid once you have tricked me outside you might flee again.
Finally.

SOPRANO ――――――――――――――――――――――――――――――――――――――

This is the matter of Webern: faith in the truth of silence, of
sunlight, ice, and alpine air, these things that appear translucent,
that are weightless and communicate lightness to us, but that, in
actuality, contain a sacred industry, invisible machinery that, rather
than producing lightness, removes encumbrance, a holy indus-
trial complex that consumes darkness. This is the source of
Webern's superiority: the luminosity of his unsolvable puzzles.

COMPOSER ――――――――――――――――――――――――――――――――――――――

The Russian stops at a Wurstelstand on the Albertinaplatz. The
Archivist lingers beneath the arcade of the opera house. Tonight
is *Lohengrin*. The Russian does not look around as he eats his
sausage and drinks his beer. The Archivist watches the Russian.

ARCHIVIST ――――――――――――――――――――――――――――――――――――――

As the long May Day parade winds its way to City Hall a protest is underway in front of the federal chancellor's office. Young Greens in orange jumpsuits and gas masks stand handcuffed together in a ring around an inflatable cooling tower, dry ice pouring out of it. Behind the tower someone cranks an old air raid siren, and it wails on and on while the group waits patiently to be arrested. The broad, curved face of the Hofburg gathers the sound and projects it out across the city, drawing spectators, tourists, sympathizers, women walking their dogs.

The Archivist follows the Russian to the Palais Ferstel, where another man, who could also be Russian, greets the Russian in front of the Café Central. They embrace and enter the café. The Archivist watches from across the street. The city's bells begin to toll the hour. He will be late for dinner with his sister and her family, across the canal in the Russian zone.

All of these can be gleaned from the simple voices of the songs—
the optimism of going home, being subsumed again into the
one soul, the possibility of reunion with the child that is, with its
lack of worldliness, so much closer to God. In this sense there is
indeed a refusal of the world, of the material, but it is the child,
not the parent, who makes the refusal, the child, rather like
Lohengrin, who is intended as the more noble, the being of
higher consciousness, communicating something of the eternal
through the flash of its eyes.

SOPRANO ——

COMPOSER ———————————————————————————————————————

ARCHIVIST ———————————————————————————————————————

The *Kindertotenlieder* are songs of eyes and light and finally, despite the turmoil of the parents' grief, of calm. Mahler's blending of these two natures is superb. They were his, of course, and it seems that he was able to reconcile them only in his musical world. A beautiful but artificial world, sadly, as with Wagner. It is extremely hard to imagine such paradises being presented with such earnestness, such intelligence today.

A weighty symbol, the siren, meant to call attention to the latest Russian bombardment. And more than that, perhaps, to the current political siege of the city. The Nazis called Vienna a fortress, and it's become one again against the forces of international public opinion. But then there's the parade, the May Day carnival in the Prater, a clear day, and the expectation of the election.

The Archivist watches his father exit the Café Central, an old man walking with a cane. The father is still counting, cautiously enunciating almost unpronounceable numerals. He crosses the street, in the direction of the Archivist, where he encounters a group of men standing on the opposite corner as if they have been waiting for him, old friends and neighbors, Austrians of a certain age, with pink faces and wrinkled necks, suits of blue and gray. Professional men, government men, family men. They all speak in numbers, in low tones, as shadows flock to them, adorn them like the ebony plumage of imperial eagles, and these men laugh now and then at the jokes encoded in their equations.

And what about a more personal refusal, perhaps one rooted in your own experience?
I've already mentioned my affinity for Mahler, for the songs.
Yes, but away from the stage...there are, have always been ru-mors....
Questions?
Questions, yes. About your own childlessness, about what you and others, including Peter Litschauer, have simply called a pro-fessional decision. Others have suggested a more detailed story, including the involvement of a rather infamous camp doctor.
Yes, I am aware of these questions. Is this how we will end? You are asking me to respond now? Again? Still?

SOPRANO ──────────────────────────────────────

The frenzy of scarlet May Day flags, of red and white flags, overwhelms Vienna as much as the grim drone of the protesters' siren. These wings of frivolity transport us to a harmless, un-touchable world of *Gemütlichkeit*, of ordinary, pleasant people, lederhosen, dirndls, Sachertorte, small automobiles, and "Rock Me Amadeus." The pleasures of sport and public transportation, the pleasure of relative insignificance, of being in the middle of things, of being without responsibility. The pleasure, the great-est pleasure of a shining blue future without consequences. Just as it's always been.

COMPOSER ──────────────────────────────────────

The Archivist shudders as the group falls silent and they turn their hard, mirror eyes on him. And now he too is speaking in numbers, counting, as are the Viennese all around him on the street, in the U-Bahn station, on the train across the canal, all the young and all the old. But the Archivist does not take medica-tion for these hallucinations, and he does not go to a therapist. To say that one has visited one's therapist in Vienna is to offer the first line of a very bad joke.

ARCHIVIST ──────────────────────────────────────

I know that there is no trusting you. And you know there is no trusting me. What more can I give you, little Lotte? What more to tempt you out of the ether into a haunting? All that is left is my voice, and I give you what little remains without regret. Take it then, my dear little horror, and promise to sing me lullabies every night. For music I have used it for the very last time.

The legend-bound world of Im Auholz 8 is only a twenty-minute train ride from the First District. All along the line modernity has struggled to emerge: graffiti, billboards, warehouses, brick and concrete communal housing, oxidizing industriana. The gigantic face of the progressive presidential candidate.

The Archivist scans the ridged plateau of the record for dust sparkling beneath the lamplight. He wants the grooves to be completely clean. He blows on the record, then scans it again. He is unsteady because he has drunk too much wine. His stomach growls because he has had no dinner.

SOPRANO ──

But the Old World, the primary branch of history, Austria's
superhistory, remains relentlessly alive as the stations continue
to pass. Sagging clothesline, horse, vineyard, cemetery. The long
sequence of grinning, *gemütlich* Waldheims lining the walls of
the subterranean center.

COMPOSER ──

The record is clean. There are no pops, no skips, no repetitions
as the particle music unwinds from its shimmering blackness, as
the names Schönberg and Berg and Webern slowly turn around
the spindle, as the Archivist lies down and closes his eyes in the
starless dark.

ARCHIVIST ──

ACKNOWLEDGMENTS

This book itself is an archive of voices, so first acknowledgements should go to those who have contributed so generously to its fabric.

Anton von Webern: A Chronicle of His Life and Work by Hans Moldenhauer and Rosaleen Moldenhauer, Knopf.

Essays on Art and Literature by Johann Wolfgang von Goethe, translated by Ellen von Nardroff and Ernest H. von Nardroff, Suhrkamp Publishers New York, Inc.

Extract from *Writings on Art* by Johann Joachim Winckelmann, edited by David Irwin, Phaidon Press 1972.

Extracts from *An Autobiographical Study* by Sigmund Freud, translated by James Strachey. Copyright 1952 by W. W. Norton & Company, Inc., renewed © 1980 by Alix Strachey. Copyright 1935 by Sigmund Freud, renewed © 1963 by James Strachey. Used by permission of W. W. Norton & Company, Inc. Translation © 1959 The Institute of Psycho-Analysis and Angela Richards, reproduced by arrangement with Paterson Marsh Ltd., London.

Extracts from *Posthumous Papers of a Living Author* by Robert Musil, translated by Peter Wortsman (first published in Germany under the title *Nachlass zu Lebzeiten* in *Gesammelte Werke* by Rowohlt Verlag GmbH, Hamburg, 1978). Copyright in *Gesammelte Werke, Neu-Edition* (edited by Adolf Frisé) © Rowohlt Verlag GmbH, Reinbek bei Hamburg, 1978. Translation copyright © Peter Wortsman, 1987. Reproduced by permission of Penguin Books Ltd.

Extracts from *The World of Yesterday* by Stefan Zweig, translated by Helmut Ripperger, copyright 1943 by the Viking Press, Inc. Used by permission of Viking Penguin, a division of Penguin Group (USA) Inc.

Extracts on pages 109-111 from *Relativity* by Albert Einstein, translated by Robert W. Lawson, Random House. © The

Hebrew University of Jerusalem.

Half-Truths and One-and-a-Half Truths: Selected Aphorisms by Karl Kraus, translated by Harry Zohn, Carcanet Press Limited, 1986.

Harmonielehre by Arnold Schönberg, translated by Roy E. Carter, University of California Press, 1978. © 1922, 1949 by Universal Edition A.G., Wien/UE 26000.

Hyperion by Friedrich Hölderlin, translated by Willard R. Trask (New York: Frederick Ungar, 1965). Adapted by David Schwarz and reprinted in *Hyperion and Selected Poems, The German Library: Volume 22*, edited by Eric L. Santer. Reprinted here by permission of The Continuum International Publishing Group.

Letters to Hildegard Jone and Josef Humplik by Anton Webern, translated by Cornelius Cardew. Original German version © 1959 by Universal Edition A.G., Wien/UE 13100. English Edition © 1967 by Theodore Presser Co., Pennsylvania/UE 14230.

The Life of Webern by Kathryn Bailey, Cambridge University Press. Reprinted with the permission of Cambridge University Press.

My Life by Leon Trotsky. Reprinted by permission of Esteban Volkow.

The Notebooks of Malte Laurids Brigge by Rainer Maria Rilke, translated by Stephen Mitchell, Vintage.

The Not Quite Innocent Bystander: Writings of Edward Steuermann, edited by Clara Steuermann, David Porter, and Gunther Schuller. Reprinted by permission of the University of Nebraska Press. Copyright © 1989 by the University of Nebraska Press.

Ornament and Crime by Adolf Loos, translated by Michael Mitchell, Ariadne Press.

The Path to the New Music by Anton Webern, translated by Leo Black. © With kind permission by Universal Edition A.G., Wien/UE 12947.

Physics and Beyond: Encounters and Conversations by Werner Heisenberg, translated by Arnold J. Pomerans. Copyright © 1971 by Harper & Row, Publishers, Inc. Reprinted

I must emphasize my indebtedness to both Webern biographies named above, the Moldenhauers' monumental work and Bailey's trimmer volume, as well as to Malcolm Hayes's *Anton von Webern*, Brigitte Hamann's *Hitler's Vienna*, and *The Annotatable Elektronic Interactive Öesterreich Universal Information System* (www.aeiou.at), which provided numerous miscellaneous details of Austrian life, history, and culture. I should also cite Pierre Boulez's interpretations of Webern's *Complete Works: Opp. 1-31*, to which I returned many times for clarity.

Many thanks to the editors of the following journals who published excerpts of this book: *3rd bed, Denver Quarterly, New Orleans Review, Quarterly West, Salt Hill, Tatlin's Tower.* Special thanks to Paul Maliszewski and M.T. Anderson for their close and thoughtful readings.

In Tuscaloosa, thanks to Michael Martone for his questions and guidance and for introducing me to FC2. Thanks also to Sandy Huss, Richard Rand, and John and Claire Keeble for their thoughtful readings, comments, and friendship. Special thanks to Marvin Johnson for his generosity with his time and musical knowledge. And thanks to the University of Alabama for providing travel and research funds.

In Shippensburg, thanks to Rich Zumkhawala-Cook at Shippensburg University for his on-air support of this book and experimental music of all stripes.

In Vienna, special thanks to Aygün Lausch and to Elisabeth Knessl of Universal Edition, Hartmut Krones of the Universität für Musik und darstellende Kunst Wien, the staff of the Arnold Schönberg Center, Hilda Stadler for her memories of the Weberns, and Doris Veit for translating and for access to the Webern home in Maria Enzersdorf. It should be noted that neither the archive nor the archivist in this book in any way resemble or are intended to resemble those I encountered in Vienna.

In Tallahassee and Normal, thanks to everyone at Fiction Collective 2, particularly Brenda Mills, Ralph Berry, and Tara Reeser.

And, finally, here and elsewhere, many thanks to my family and to Mindy and Napoleon for all your love, patience, and support.